Readers love
SCOTTY CADE

Forever For Now

"Scotty Cade is usually good for a sweet low-angst story with a guaranteed happily ever after, and *Forever for Now* is no exception."
—Prism Book Alliance

"…a good choice if you are looking for a quick, sexy read. You'll enjoy the heroes' chemistry and it has an ending that will leave a smile on your face."
—Top 2 Bottom Reviews

"…a sweet romantic story that showcased this writer's ability to create vivid characters and moments of tension and angst that only added to the story. A sweet read for those looking to escape for just a little while."
—The Novel Approach

After the Final Encore

"…this isn't the type of book that you sit back and psychoanalyse; simply enjoy it for what it is."
—MM Good Book Reviews

Veiled Loyalties

"I think that if you like mysteries with a romantic bent—this is your story/series…"
—The Blogger Girls

"The writing was flawless and the story well thought out. The characters were just absolutely amazing and the story was one I just could not put down."
—Inked Rainbow Reviews

By SCOTTY CADE

Acting Out
Forever for Now
The Mystery of Ruby Lode
Sunrise Over Savannah • Chasing the Horizon
An Unconventional Courtship • An Unconventional Union

BISSONET & CRUZ INVESTIGATIONS
The Royal Street Heist
Veiled Loyalties

FINAL ENCORE
Before the Final Encore
Final Encore
After the Final Encore

LOVE SERIES
Wings of Love
Bounty of Love
Treasure of Love
With Z.B. Marshall: Foundation of Love

Published by DREAMSPINNER PRESS
www.dreamspinnerpress.com

KNOBS

SCOTTY CADE

Published by

DREAMSPINNER PRESS

5032 Capital Circle SW, Suite 2, PMB# 279, Tallahassee, FL 32305-7886 USA
www.dreamspinnerpress.com/

Knobs
© 2016 Scotty Cade.

Cover Art
© 2016 Reese Dante.
http://www.reesedante.com
Cover content is for illustrative purposes only and any person depicted on the cover is a model.

ISBN: 978-1-63477-123-8
Digital ISBN: 978-1-63477-124-5
Library of Congress Control Number: 2015920424
Published April 2016
v. 1.0

Printed in the United States of America
∞
This paper meets the requirements of
ANSI/NISO Z39.48-1992 (Permanence of Paper).

First and foremost, as with everything I write, this novel is dedicated to Kell, my hero and husband of only two years, but my best friend and life partner for over the last twenty years.

It seems like just yesterday I spotted you up on a ladder in your Daisy Duke cutoffs, cleaning out your gutters, and once I got the courage to stop and introduce myself, well, let's just say, "The rest is history." You are my first thought when I open my eyes each morning and my last thought when I close them at night. Every book I write has a part of you, me, and us embedded deep within the pages. I love you with all my heart and couldn't begin to imagine my life without you in it. Thank you for your continued support and encouragement. Always!

Also to my BFF, SJD "Jo" Peterson, who was the original voice behind Stewart Adam Morley. We've always wanted to write a story together and started working on this book as coauthors four years ago. But as close as we are as BFFs, our writing voices didn't mesh very well. Since I was so close to this story, having spent a great deal of time at the Citadel and observing so many of these rituals first hand, she unselfishly relinquished the story to me with her blessings. Jo, I hope I did Sam proud. XOXO

And last, but certainly not least, to my friend and editor Andi Byassee. The way you take my literary children and force their words to make sense amazes me. Each book I write has a small part of my life embedded in the pages, and you instinctively know what those parts are, what to leave alone, and what to make better. But the most important thing is, when everything is said and done, the expressions on the pages are all mine. My voice and my words. Thank you from the bottom of my heart. XOXO

PREFACE

HELLO, ALL. Scotty here. I wanted to chat just a little before you join me on this journey. As I mentioned in the dedications, my BFF, SJD "Jo" Peterson, and I started out writing this book together. Kell and I were spending the winter on our boat at the Charleston City Marina, and the Citadel is walking distance from the marina, so I got to spend quite a bit of time on campus. I worked out at the gym, played racquetball at Deas Hall, and attended many of the Friday afternoon parades. Until Jo got here and saw it all for herself, I sent her endless photos and videos for her to get the feel of the place. The camaraderie was everywhere, and I literally got chills each Friday when I saw the parades. The marching, the cannons going off, the bagpipers. It was all just so overwhelming and emotional. Not to mention getting to watch hundreds of cadets in uniform covering the campus. Sorry. I digress.

Anyway when Jo arrived for a visit, we spent time walking the campus and observing all we could to make this book as real as possible: getting building locations right and most of all learning all we could about Hell Week.

But with all that said, the tough part about writing this book was the fact that no matter how wonderful the Citadel and the incredible men and women they release into the world are, "gay" is not a part of the curriculum there. From what I could gather, there are always a few gay people who attend, but they were never out or able to be themselves on or off campus.

Don't get me wrong, I don't mean gay men or women should walk the campus holding hands or making out, because none of that is acceptable whether gay or straight, but I just wish they were able to at least be acknowledged, supported, and embraced for who and what they are. Not that sexuality defines us, but it is part of who we are. Who knows? Maybe one day it will.

So in closing, just keep in mind the restraints surrounding these characters and how they struggled to just "be."

I hope you enjoy!

PART ONE

CHAPTER ONE
LEAVING BEHIND THE COMFORTS OF HOME

Stewart Adam Morley - Sam

SITTING OUTSIDE the Greyhound terminal, Sam fought to keep down the bile burning his throat. The offensive smell of diesel, billowing around him in thick clouds, was only part of what was causing his stomach to roll. He was about to step onto a bus that would take him away from everything and everyone he knew, leaving behind the comforts and familiarity of home.

Growing up in Southfield, just outside of Detroit, wasn't always what he'd call comfortable. While some of the areas were nice, the block he'd grown up on wasn't the safest. However, he knew the streets, knew what areas to avoid, and once he was behind the multiple locks on his front door, enjoyed a sense of security only home could provide.

He knew nothing about Charleston, South Carolina. The people were all strangers, the streets unfamiliar. Yet it would be his home for the next four years.

If I survive.

Yeah, that unnerving thought had played in his head a time or two or a hundred.

Sam leaned his head against the brick wall and closed his eyes as the nausea increased. He clutched his backpack in his trembling hands, his two duffel bags piled securely next to his feet. Jesus, what the hell had he been thinking when he'd accepted that damn football scholarship?

He'd been offered both academic and athletic scholarships to numerous colleges and universities around the country. Originally he'd turned them all down—too damn scared, too unsure—and chosen to attend the local community college. He'd taken the easy route, the safe one that was closer to home. However, his dream of attending the Citadel Military College, which began when he'd first seen a pamphlet one of the seniors had been tossing around during Sam's freshman year, kept nagging at him. It refused to be silenced. He'd worked his ass off to keep his grade point average high, had a record year on the field as a senior, and after a year and a half of hemming and hawing, was thankful the Citadel was still interested enough in him playing for the Bulldogs to offer him a scholarship. *Nothing like taking the road most challenging*, he thought with a sigh.

"Greyhound 1125. Final destination Charleston, South Carolina. Now boarding."

The announcement had Sam taking a deep breath, getting to his feet, and again wrinkling his nose at the horrible smell around him. He shouldered his backpack, grabbed his two duffel bags, and fell in line behind those rushing for the bus, his steps heavy and sluggish. He wasn't in any hurry to start the twenty-four-hour ride. It wasn't that he didn't want to begin the next journey of his life. He did, and knew he was making the right choice. But he was still going to miss his mom, his brother and sister—even if they were pains in the ass sometimes—and his friends.

Don't go. Just turn around and go home.

Sam hesitated for a long moment, again questioning what the hell he was doing, his head filled with doubt. The known versus the unknown, the easy versus the hard; the same battle he'd been fighting for the last year and a half. But like every other time he'd had these thoughts, the challenge was too exciting, too alluring, to ignore. He shoved that little voice away, pushed past the fear and doubt, and handed his ticket and duffel bags to the attendant.

"No turning back now," he whispered to himself.

He'd never been away from home, and the anxiety over leaving what he knew wasn't the only thing weighing heavily on him. He was twenty, and it was time, but the thought of his mom having to care for his younger siblings and herself without him around was daunting. He was the man of the house. He'd taken on that role at twelve when his stepdad had followed in the shoes of his real dad and split. No note, no forwarding address, just gone. Well, back then they hadn't needed the lazy bastard. His mom and siblings had him. But now he was also leaving. Not like his father and stepdad had, but he was leaving all the same. It didn't matter how many times Mom had tried to convince him otherwise, he felt like he was abandoning his family, his responsibilities, and it sucked. Down in the pit of his gut and the center of his chest, it sucked.

Sam found himself a seat toward the back of the bus, relieved when it looked as if he'd have the entire row to himself—at least on this leg of the journey. He popped in his earbuds and turned up the volume on his used iPod, a going-away gift from his mom, letting the soothing sounds of Joshua James help ease the panic that still gripped him. Taking in a deep breath through his nose, Sam let it out slowly through his slightly parted lips. He leaned his head against the window as the bus slowly pulled away from the terminal. The trepidation that had kept him from sleeping the night before, leaving him exhausted, combined with the rambling, rhythmic movements of the bus, made it impossible to keep his eyes open, and blessedly his brain shut down. He wrapped his arms around his backpack, head resting against the cool glass, and slipped into a fitful sleep before the bus even made it out of the city.

MOVING HESITANTLY, Sam walked through the archway that led to the center and heart of the Citadel campus. Twilight cast eerie shadows on Summerall Field, or the parade deck as it was frequently called. His pulse raced and even in the stifling heat, a chill ran down his spine. Sam wrapped his arms around his chest and forced his feet to keep moving. He could feel the icy tendrils of fear gripping him, the adrenaline pumping through his veins, demanding he flee, but something stronger compelled him forward. Men with shaved heads—dressed smartly in full-dress wool jackets, white trousers, spit-shined leather shoes, and cross belts forming bright white X's across their chests connected to a cartridge box—marched silently past him. In one white-gloved hand, they held their weapons against their shoulders. To Sam's horror, each one turned hollow eyes on him and pointed at him as they passed. The contempt on their hard faces made him shudder.

The grass was cool and lush beneath his feet as Sam rushed past the parading cadets, and for the first time, he realized his feet were bare. Not only was he shoeless, his pants were torn and filthy, as was his T-shirt. A sour odor emanated from his clothing, much like the stench of rotting garbage. He wiped his palms across the front of his shirt as he fled, trying to wipe away the dirt, only to find his hands were covered in filth and his actions doing little more than increasing the size of the stains. He looked and smelled worse than some of the homeless men he'd encountered back home in the downtown area. No wonder the cadets were so disgusted.

Keeping his head down, Sam moved quickly across the grounds. He'd been here before—he recognized the six-foot replica of the Citadel graduates' class ring—but in the dusk it looked foreign, almost like a large humpbacked creature, poised to strike. The flags upon the tall poles flanking the east perimeter waved wildly, their shadows making the ground seem as if it had come alive, yet no wind blew. Keep moving. Go, go, go, a voice in his head screamed. You don't belong here. *Sam quickened his pace, ran past men in blue T-shirts and blue shorts with neon-yellow belts who stopped when they saw him to point and sneer. Go!*

As Sam reached the center of the field, he stopped dead in his tracks. Not like hitting a barrier, stopping his forward motion, but rather as if he were suddenly glued to the spot. The hair on the back of his neck stood on end, and his heart hammered painfully as he scanned the area around him. A military vehicle sat in each corner. Tanks, a helicopter, a fighter jet—all pointed toward him, targeting him. Sam couldn't see the occupants of the vehicles, but somehow he knew they were there, staring at him, pointing and sneering as the others had done. Sam jerked when a flash of light lit up the field. The men around him began to chant, too low for Sam to make out, but the tone was ominous.

"Ready," a voice boomed from near a row of cannons.

The chant grew louder but remained incoherent.

"Set."

"You don't belong here." Glowing eyes surrounded the parade field. "You don't belong here."

"Fire!"

The ground shook with the force of the explosion, the noise deafening, and Sam covered his ears and screamed.

Sam jerked awake and scanned the area with wild eyes, his breath coming in painful gasps. The woman in the next row was looking down at the knitting in her hands; the gentleman next to her appeared to be sleeping.

"Oh God! Just a dream," he muttered and slumped back against the seat, working to get his pounding heart and rapid breathing to return to normal.

It wasn't the first time he'd had the dream. Since visiting the campus back in April, he'd woken numerous times to the same explosion of cannon fire. He also knew the meaning behind it, and he was bound and determined to prove it wrong. He might be poor, a little unrefined, perhaps too brash, but he *did* belong at the Citadel.

Lying back, Sam closed his eyes. The dream still held him in its clutches. Flashes of hollow eyes and pointing, laughing figures danced behind his lids. He forced himself to relax, push down the unease, and focus on the positive. Sam turned up the volume on his iPod and lost himself in the slow rhythmic beat. It took a while, but he finally fell into a deep sleep—this time, void of nightmares.

One transfer in Cincinnati, Ohio, another in Knoxville, Tennessee, forced Sam to rouse, but other than that, he slept. Blessedly the nightmare didn't return to haunt him. The entire trip was a blur, and the next thing he knew, he was sitting on a bed in a run-down hotel a block from the bus terminal, staring at… well, nothing at all really. Just staring.

Sam ran a hand through his hair and fingered the strands between his fingers. His stomach went all jittery when a thought crossed his mind. The nervous habit he had of playing with his hair wasn't going to be an option for much longer. Not only would he be losing his civilian clothes when he entered the Citadel tomorrow, but his shaggy auburn locks as well. His hair would be cut to within a quarter inch of his scalp, and whether he'd be able to handle being a Knob or not, he sure as hell was going to look like one.

His chest tightened painfully, and he closed his eyes as he struggled with the new surge of panic that threatened to steal his breath.

Breathe in deeply…. Hold it…. Now let it out slowly. And again.

Sam repeated the mantra several times until he was able to calm down and take a lungful of air without having to work for it. Jesus, he was turning into a pansy. How the hell was he going to make it through the first week if he was going to freak out over something as simple as a haircut? It was just hair for Christ's sake. It'd grow back.

Sam shook his head, doing a little mental chastising of his internal scaredy-cat. Or maybe it was his vanity that had him freaking over the loss of his hair. As he studied his reflection in the mirror hanging on the wall across from him, he realized this particular anxiety attack was indeed all about his vanity.

"So much for my pretty boy looks," he muttered and pushed himself up from the mattress. Either way, he'd better get a grip on his crazy, or he'd be returning home before he could make it through the first week.

Grabbing one of his duffel bags from the floor, he set it on the small desk and opened it. He might as well do something to keep his mind occupied. After napping for the majority of his twenty-four-hour ride from Michigan, he doubted if he'd be able to get any sleep. As he pulled the contents from his duffel, he counted out six white crew-neck T-shirts, which he shook out and refolded before setting them on the bed. Next he pulled out twelve pairs of boxers, black crew socks, and white cotton athletic socks and stacked them on the bed along with the other items. It had been a struggle to purchase everything he needed to take to his new home, and he'd had to pick up extra shifts at the deli to manage it. Although his mom had offered to get everything he needed, he simply couldn't allow her to. And he was glad he hadn't, especially since she'd loaded up a ton of minutes on a prepaid cell phone for him.

The items on his list he was required to bring would have cost her an entire two weeks' salary. She was already working two jobs and barely made enough money to get by. Instead he'd bought not only the clothes, boots, and shoes set out in the handbook, but also bath towels, washcloths, a pillow, pillow cases, four nonfitted white sheets, and twelve white handkerchiefs. He knew exactly how many items he had. He'd checked and double-checked them against the list the day before. With a disgusted sigh, he shoved everything back into his duffel.

Sam flopped down on the bed, threw an arm over his eyes, and groaned. While the nausea had subsided and the panic from earlier dissipated, he was now bored and, worse still, lonely. Damn, he wished he could call his best friend, Chris. Unfortunately he had to save the allotted minutes on his phone to keep in contact with his mom.

He briefly considered venturing out and visiting the city, but he had no clue where he would go. Still six months until he could drink legally, limited cash, and honestly, wandering around aimlessly would probably only exacerbate the loneliness.

"Screw it," he grumbled. He grabbed the remote and hit the power button. He wasn't alone; he had mind-numbing television to keep him company.

At some point the wearingly dull, repetitive, and snooze-inducing infomercials did their job, and the next thing Sam knew, he was blinking against the rising sun streaming through the windows of his small hotel room. He yawned and then stretched, his body protesting the inactivity over the last two days with a series of pops and snaps. He rubbed his eyes, got up, and headed to the shower. Time to get this adventure started.

IT SEEMED like ages had passed from sweating through the first interview, to getting his physical examination, to receiving the acceptance letter, and finally, to arriving on the campus of the Citadel. It was the morning of August 1, and here he was, standing in the parking lot at Johnson Hagood Stadium, clean-shaven and arms full of the few items allowed in the barracks.

The Citadel wasn't near as crowded as Sam had imagined because the Citadel athletes, the Corps Squad as they were called, started their first semester and Hell Week one week earlier than the other cadets so they could begin practicing their sport when the regular semester began.

"Name?" a cadet asked.

"Sam... I mean, Stewart Adam Morley," he responded nervously.

The mild anxiety he'd felt when he'd woken was now ramping up as he was handed a packet and given directions to his assigned barracks and company in a cold monotone voice from a cadet who barely looked at him. Not the warmest welcome he'd ever received. The campus was intimidating as hell in and of itself. Throw in the fact that he seemed to be the only new cadet who had no family with him, and he felt as if he were already being singled out as the outcast. No one said a word to Sam as he moved sluggishly along the sidewalk toward his barracks. The outcast feeling was a product of his own insecurities, of course. However, he knew at least on some level it must be true. How could it not be? All around him young men walked with their parents, their wealth obvious in the luxury cars they'd arrived in and the expensive appearance of their clothing. Sam could see it in their walk and in the way they held themselves, adding to Sam's feeling of inferiority.

The one good thing about the morning was that it happened fast, in a blur of "go here," "report there," and "drop your bags in there," giving Sam little time to dwell on his apprehension—or outright panic. He was told where to go and when, and he followed along without conscious thought, keeping his head down and his ears open.

Sam surrendered his civilian clothes and changed into the blue T-shirt, blue shorts, and neon-yellow belt he'd be wearing every morning for Physical Training, or PT as they called it. Once sporting the proper attire and with his CamelBak hydration system around his neck, he arrived in the hall a few minutes early. At 0800 hours the Academic Officer gave Sam and the others who'd been assigned to the Fourth Battalion, Tango Company, a tour of the campus. He was reminded once again by the magnificent buildings, the grandeur of the gardens, and the pristine condition of the campus that he was out of his league. He was a poor kid from the wrong side of the tracks who had been blessed with the ability to play a game and play it well. But that did little to help him feel as if he would ever fit in.

The tour ended back at the main hall. Sweat rolled down his spine and dripped into his eyes, causing them to burn in the stifling heat. The ungodly hot temperature of the South was a fitting backdrop because suddenly all hell broke loose.

The next phase of his introduction was the Cadre. He'd read about the group of cadets—made up of mainly juniors, some sophomores and a few seniors—who were forced to come back from summer break early to help train the Knobs. And from the looks on their faces, they didn't seem very happy about it. There were about fifteen to twenty Cadre for every twenty or thirty Knobs, and they were all lined up, throwing uniforms at them and screaming. Constantly screaming. It was disorienting, but Sam followed along, flinching each time he was shoved or something was shoved at him.

He'd watched quite a few military documentaries, and the Cadre was very much like the sergeants he'd seen screaming and yelling at the new arrivals to boot camp. Which, come to think of it, shouldn't shock him. He was, after all, currently on the campus of the finest military college in the United States. The thought was sobering. Amid the chaos Col. Martin R. Taylor was a constant presence. He was the Fourth Battalion's TAC or Battalion Tactical Officer. He was the "adult" who any cadets who couldn't take Hell Week could walk up to and quit. Although his heart was racing, his palms were sweaty, and he was frickin' freaked out, Sam had no plans to ever utter those words—to the TAC officer or anyone else.

Quitting was not an option. It was the coward's way out, and he was no damn coward.

Back in April when he'd visited the Citadel before making the choice to accept the scholarship, he'd been given some great advice from one of the upperclassmen. "Keep a good attitude, do what you are asked, stay focused, and realize that if your Cadre can do it, so can you." Sam knew if he kept that advice close, he'd make it through this.

Sam had never been one to think too much about what he wore. Between family, studies, work, and football, he hadn't had the energy or the desire to be a trendsetter. T-shirt, jeans, and running shoes were about the extent of his fashion sense. Still, he loved his hair. He was just vain enough that as he stood there watching the other new arrivals getting up from the chair with horror-stricken looks on their faces, rubbing their newly shaved heads, he was vibrating, resisting the fight or flight response surging through him.

Forcing his feet to move a step closer, he repeated his mantra. *If your Cadre can do it, so can you.*

He slid into the seat and a black cape was immediately draped around him. He saw the clippers coming toward him and dug his fingers into the vinyl arms of the chair to keep himself from bolting.

If your Cadre can do it, so can you. If your Cadre can do it, so can you, he recited mentally, over and over again.

He tightened his grip and shut his eyes when he heard the buzzing sound of the clippers, and he flinched when they touched the top of his head, but he swallowed hard and forced himself to stillness.

If your Cadre can do it, so can you.

He continued repeating the words until the sound of the clippers died and the cape was pulled away. When Sam opened his eyes, he caught his reflection in the mirror and ran a hand over his scalp, doing his best not to laugh at the Knob staring back at him.

CHAPTER TWO
PUSHED TO THE LIMIT: HELL WEEK

ONE OF the things that had appealed to Sam about the Citadel was what was called the fourth class system, something all the service academies had at one time. Instead of four years of leadership development, the Citadel tortured you as much as possible during the freshman, or Knob, year. Sort of like plebes/rats at other military schools but considerably more intense as all the energy of the second and first classes focused on it. The third class joined in during the second semester to make life even more miserable. But the system meant only one year of hell instead of four. At least that was what Sam kept telling himself. At most other schools, after the first semester of each year, things calmed down, but at the Citadel every day apparently brought the same insane pressure. Only for your first year, though.

Jesus, was he delusional?

Exhausted, his neck sore from holding his chin to his chest all day, Sam crawled into his bed and pulled the covers up over his head. He only had about five hours before he had to be up, dressed in his PT clothes, and at McAlister Field House. No problem, he was falling into the darkness of sleep before his head even finished settling into his pillow, and as such he would be taking advantage of the full five hours.

A loud noise like someone kicking in a door jerked Sam into a sitting position.

"Get up! Get your asses out of those beds. Feet on the floor, Knobs!"

Dazed and confused, he blinked rapidly as he waited for his eyes to adjust to the harsh fluorescent light that flooded the barracks. Sam's heart hammered, nearly leaping out of his chest as he did his best to figure out what the fuck was going on.

"Move, move, move," another voice screamed.

Throwing off the covers, Sam got to his feet as he was told and tried to get a handle on what the hell was happening. Two upperclassmen were pulling clothes out of dressers and closets, a flurry of white socks, T-shirts, and boxers flying around the room. A third was pulling his bunkmate out of his cot.

"Drop and give me twenty. Now! Now! Now! Do it!"

Sam glanced up at the clock—0300 hours—and gritted his teeth. *So much for five hours of sleep.*

"You." One of the cadets who'd been pulling things from the dresser poked Sam hard in the chest. "Pick this shit up. Now! Do it!"

Without a word, keeping the pressure on his jaw to keep the snarky comment that threatened from passing his lips, Sam quickly gathered up the discarded clothing and began shoving them back into the drawers.

"What the hell are you doing?" the cadet screamed, getting right in Sam's face. His breath stunk of coffee. He slapped the clothing out of Sam's hands. "Don't you dare shove them back in the drawers like that. What the hell are you, a pig? Drop and give me twenty." The man sneered.

No, obviously I'm a monkey. Sam didn't say it out loud—although the urge was strong—he simply nodded.

"Oh, you're a fucking deaf-mute."

"No, sir."

The man leaned in till their noses were practically touching. "Then you show me a little respect, or I will make your life a living hell. Is that understood, Knob?"

"Yes, sir."

"Now do as you're told and drop!"

Dropping to the floor, Sam counted off twenty, keeping his eyes on the shiny black shoes just beneath his face. After he completed the last push-up, he stood, pressed his chin to his chest, and waited.

"Now, little piggy, let's try picking this shit up again, shall we?"

"Yes, sir."

Sam picked up a T-shirt from the floor, carefully folded it, and placed it on his bunk. As he continued to fold the strewn clothing, he kept his head down and his mouth shut. Greg Cummings, his bunkmate, wasn't so smart.

When one of the cadets started going through Greg's personal belongings, Greg went off on him. "Hey! What the hell do you think you're doing? That's against policy."

Sam didn't stop what he was doing, but he watched with interest out of the corner of his eye.

"I make the policies, so shut the hell up and give me twenty."

From where Sam stood, he could see Greg literally vibrating with anger. Greg opened his mouth to protest, but luckily before anything came out, he snapped it shut again. He reluctantly did as he was told and gave the cadet twenty as the man continued to rummage through his belongings.

And then they were gone.

Thirty minutes of screaming and stuff flying around and push-ups and insanity, and then it was just over. The three upperclassmen, as if they'd been on a timer and the alarm had sounded, suddenly stopped what they were doing, spun on their heels, and left the room. The silence was a little unnerving, and it was obvious from the incredulous look on Greg's face that he was feeling it too. The two of them stood there as if they were trying to figure out what had just happened. For a long moment, they did nothing but stare at the closed door as if they expected it to fly open again.

"WHAT IN the hell," Greg bellowed, coming out of his stupor and pointing toward the door, "was that?"

"I do believe that was our welcoming committee," Sam told him with a shrug.

Greg gaped at him. "More like someone forgot to lock the gates on the hounds of hell."

"Or that." Sam chuckled as he picked up an armful of folded clothes. "Let's get this shit put away while the dogs are distracted."

Greg stood with his hands on his hips, shaking his head. "That Speakerman guy is a real jerk," he complained and finally started helping with the clothes. "I hear this crap happens at least once a week, sometimes more. Depends on how bad his insomnia is. Likes to take the shit out on the Knobs."

"Great. Just frickin' great!" Sam muttered. Day two had sucked worse than day one. He couldn't wait to see what kind of fun day three would throw at him.

He shouldn't have been so eager.

DAY THREE, in keeping with the pattern, sucked worse than the day before and was ten times suckier than the first day. After he and Greg finally got their clothes sorted out and returned to the proper dressers and closets, it was around 4:00 a.m. Sam should have stayed awake since the sound of the alarm blaring an hour later pissed him off to no end and set his mood for the day.

Forcing himself from his bed, Sam grabbed his PT clothes and listlessly made his way toward the shower. He stood under the hot flow, letting the pulsing water land on the back of his aching neck. The whole chin to chest thing was dumb. Not only that, it was a major pain, both physically and practically. It was hard to see in that position, and twice while hurrying from the mess hall to the parade grounds, he'd run into someone who had stopped abruptly in front of him. He didn't see the point of the rule. It made zero sense, and it was… stupid.

Sam snatched the bar of soap from his mesh shower bag and ran it over his head and then to the back of his neck. He rolled his shoulders, the bones cracking and popping numerous times, but the tension began to ease a little under the constant flow of hot water. He moved downward, washing his body quickly, spending a little extra time on his tense thighs and sore calves, caused by the "hurrying." That wasn't the technical term, but Sam had no idea what else to call it. It wasn't really a march. It wasn't running. It was synchronized hurrying. But as a Knob, it was the way he had to move everywhere he went, upperclassmen constantly screaming at him, along with the other guys in his battalion, to hurry, hurry, hurry. Move, move, move.

Three days at the Citadel and he already looked, moved, and felt like a Knob.

Shutting off the taps, Sam quickly dried off and slipped into his PT clothes. He had fifteen minutes before he had to be in line for Physical Training.

"Move, move, move. Hurry, hurry, hurry," he muttered sarcastically.

BY SUPPER, Sam could barely keep his eyes open, and it was a real struggle to lift a spoonful of mashed potatoes to his mouth. What little energy he had left was used to make sure he was sitting precisely on only three inches of his chair with his spine perfectly straight and upright. Anything beyond that wasn't quite as important, including food, even if his stomach was growling and saying otherwise. After morning PT and breakfast, he'd been ordered to report to the athletic department. Between PT, Military Training, and three hours of ball practice, he was done. Put a fork in him done!

"Time for... stump the stars!" an unfamiliar voice yelled.

An upperclassman was standing near his table. His tone was like that of a game show host, but Sam ignored the irritating sound. He could care less about games. Instead, he concentrated on getting the potatoes into his mouth without dropping them down the front of his uniform.

"You," the cadet/game show host bellowed.

Without looking up, Sam jumped when hands slammed down on the table in front of him. Dammit, there went the potatoes. He picked up the mess from his lap and dropped it onto his plate.

He met the hard gaze of the cadet. "Yes, sir."

"Governor John P. Richardson first conceived of converting the Arsenal in Columbia and the Citadel in Charleston into military academies. This was accomplished by an act of the state legislature on...?"

The cadet looked at him expectantly, but Sam's exhausted brain was having a difficult time comprehending what the hell the guy was talking about. He couldn't eat his goddamn potatoes. How the Christ was he supposed to understand what was being asked of him?

"Three.... Two.... On—"

"December 20, 1842," Sam blurted out at the last moment.

The cadet scowled and abruptly spun on his heels.

Sam's shoulders slumped in relief, but he quickly righted his posture. No way was he going to do anything that might have him expending unnecessary energy now. *December 20, 1842.* Where the hell had that little tidbit come from? Obviously he'd read it somewhere, but damned if he could remember, and he really didn't care. He was just glad it was the right answer and that he wouldn't be doing push-ups.

He looked to his left as the loud voice continued to bellow through the mess hall. Greg obviously hadn't been as fortunate as Sam since he was currently on the mess hall floor, counting off twenty.

ONE MORE day of Hell Week. Sam's mantra of *if your Cadre can do it, so can you* was now being answered by another voice in his head saying *piss off*. He was tired, sore, and he wanted to talk to his mom, Chris, his little brother, Kory, or his sister, Jenny. Hell, at that point he'd settle for chatting with the crazy cat lady who used to come into the deli every Saturday and talk his fool ear off. Anyone from home would do. He felt as if he were sloshing around in some foreign universe, and while there were tons of people around—most of whom were up in his face screaming and telling him what to do—he'd never felt so alone in his life.

The cell phone in his pocket was almost a cruel joke. The Citadel had a policy forbidding Knobs from using a phone or a computer for the first two weeks of the semester, but ever since the shooting at Virginia Tech, they were allowed to have a cell phone. They just couldn't use it unless it was an absolute emergency. As he "hurried" from the mess hall, his hand brushed against the phone in his pocket. He was so tempted to find a bathroom stall with a working lock and dial his mom's number. If he could just hear her voice....

"Move, move, move. Let's go, Knobs! I don't have all day."

Sam's hand fell away from his pocket, and he rushed back to his barracks.

As he hustled, chin to chest, along the designated lane for Knobs, he realized it was only 8:00 a.m., and he'd already been up, done PT, showered, and had breakfast. Once he got back to the barracks, he'd have less than an hour to clean his bunk, shine his shoes, and get to the field for weapons training, and after that football practice. He knew he'd have little time to dwell on how lonely he felt, which was a good thing. When he finally reached his barracks, he found Greg packing his things.

"Hey, what's going on, man?"

"I'm done!" Greg growled and shoved more clothes into his pack.

"What the hell do you mean *you're done*? Done with what?"

Greg looked up at him with a hard glare. "I'm packing my fucking clothes. What does that tell you, genius?"

"Whoa, wait a minute," Sam replied and held up his hands in a defensive gesture. "Don't turn on me, man. It was a simple question."

The anger drained out of Greg's face, his shoulders slumped, and he lowered his eyes. "Sorry," he said with a sigh. He stood still for a moment and then resumed packing without looking up. "I talked to Colonel Taylor."

"You quit?" Sam asked incredulously. "We only have two more days of Hell Week. You can do this, Greg."

Greg shook his head again. "No, I can't. I don't want to. Not anymore."

"Greg, c'mon, dude."

Greg looked up once again at Sam, his eyes glistening with tears. "I never wanted to come here in the first place. My dad insisted and… he's going to be pissed, but I can't—"

"You can," Sam said, walking over to him and gently resting a hand on his shoulder. The human touch felt odd, but strangely comforting. He suddenly realized this was the first human contact he'd had since he'd had his head shaved.

Greg tensed briefly, and Sam removed his hand. Greg huffed out a breath and closed his now stuffed duffel bag. "Let me rephrase that. I don't want to do this. Like I said, my dad will be pissed, but he'll just have to deal." He gave Sam a small smile. After shouldering his bag, Greg stepped up close and extended his hand.

"Are you sure?" Sam asked.

"I'm sure. Good luck, dude."

"Thanks, man. Same to you."

He shook the offered hand and watched as Greg strode out of the room. He didn't know Greg all that well, but he was at least a familiar face. Now Sam really was completely alone.

He pushed through the unease he felt over Greg's departure and did the best he could to get through his chores. Within the hour, with his shoes spit-shined, his room in perfect order, and his uniform ready, Sam headed down to the communal barracks, or the squad room as it was called. The squad room was more like some poor Knob's room that had been designated as the meeting place. He didn't know who had chosen that particular room; he was only thankful it hadn't been his. Everyone just kind of met up there to talk, bitch, complain, and check each other over to make sure their uniforms and shoes were up to snuff before every formation or whatever chore or task was next on their agenda. That many guys crowding into a room ensured it was always in disarray, and quite frankly it smelled like dirty socks, but he was grateful for the chance to see and hear he wasn't alone in all of this.

The squad room was exceptionally crowded when Sam walked in. Tomorrow, as part of the Corps Squad, his Hell Week would be over and the "regular" Knobs would officially begin theirs. Chuckling, Sam squeezed past a group of guys complaining about Speakerman and his nightly insomniac raid. He really shouldn't laugh, but what else could you do? Besides, better them than him.

One more day! he thought as he pressed up against the wall toward the back, waiting for his turn to be inspected. Not that he had any illusions the next week would be better, or even the next year. But he'd endured the harshest week, and that was something to be proud of. After the inspecting cadet gave him the thumbs-up, he headed for the door. He stopped when he saw a group of new cadets and their parents on a tour of the campus. *Poor guys. They have no idea what to expect: shaved heads, Hell Week. Welcome to the Citadel, boys.*

One new cadet hung back, and he grabbed Sam's attention and held it. As the others passed with their parents at their sides, this cadet was alone, much like Sam had been when he arrived. The new cadet stopped near the door, towering over everyone else. Jesus, the kid had to be at least six-three, maybe even six-five. He had brownish-blond hair and his wide unblinking stare revealed steel-gray eyes. Not only was he tall, he was big as well. He had a thick muscular chest that tapered down to a lean waist. One word came to mind—*hot.* The thought was unnerving.

Sam turned away. He had no business thinking those kinds of things. Not here. Not for the next four years.

CHAPTER THREE
FULFILLING A LEGACY

Angus Conrad McRae III - Gus

ANGUS CONRAD McRae III, Gus to everyone but his family, checked and rechecked the required clothing spread across his bed in neat piles. He sighed, stepped back, and leaned against his desk, nervously crossing his arms over his chest. His heart started to race, a chill ran down his spine, and he felt weak in the knees. *My God, this is really happening!*

Tomorrow morning at 0700 hours, he was following in his father's and his grandfather's footsteps and reporting to the Citadel as a Knob. He looked at the piles of clothing, and the reality hit him hard. He was suddenly cold, his skin damp and clammy to the touch. Gus dropped to his desk chair, fear or anticipation or both stealing away his strength.

In the solitude of his bedroom, with no prying eyes and no pretenses to keep up, he lowered his defenses and allowed himself a rare moment to doubt that he could really pull this off. Staring at his bed and shaking his head, Gus's mind raced. *This stuff is going to be my life for the next four years.* He brought his hands to his face and rubbed his eyes, the same eyes from which he was so diligently trying to keep the nervous tears at bay. He chuckled anxiously to keep from crying. *Well, that's not completely true. This stuff along with grueling physical training and an impossible academics schedule— that will be my life.* Determined to be strong, he got to his feet. His knees threatened to give way again, but he fought past the sensation and paced back and forth. Another realization hit him hard, and his stomach started to churn. *Hell Week! I've got to get through Hell Week first. What if I can't cut it? Fucking Hell Week!*

From everything he'd read and the stories his father and grandfather had told him, Hell Week was going to be a nightmare. It was designed to break down the cadets and strip away every bit of their identity and individuality until everyone was equal. The Citadel attempted to destroy the cadets' confidence, physically and mentally, based on the premise that they couldn't start to make leaders out of their young trainees until they first broke them down to a common "nothing."

Gus's hands started to shake slightly. He stopped pacing, pushed a pile of clothing aside, and sat on the foot of one of his twin beds. There he rested his elbows on his knees and covered his face with his hands. Gus rubbed his eyes again until they were about to pop out of his head.

"Stop it," he whispered. "You'll make it through Hell Week. You've been groomed for this your entire life."

A little voice in the back of Gus's head chimed in again. *Yeah, you've been groomed for this, but because of that fucking accident, you're starting a year behind everyone else and probably not near as fit.*

One Saturday morning shortly after his senior year had started, Gus had been out four-wheeling on James Island with a couple of his friends when, in a very stupid move, he caught the dunes just right—or wrong, depending on how you looked at it—and rolled his four-wheeler several times, finally coming to a stop with the thing on top of him. He cringed, remembering the excruciating pain and the sound of his bones cracking with each violent flip. The attending police officer had said if he hadn't been wearing his seatbelt, he might have been thrown clear, but the loosely fitting belt kept him attached to the vehicle as he thrashed with each roll.

Because of one stupid mistake, he'd spent his entire senior year in a full-body cast, often heavily sedated, and having to endure multiple surgeries to put him back together. And because of that single moment in time, he'd had to retake his senior year while suffering through grueling physical therapy in order to get back into shape and be able to attend the Citadel. The worse part was that all of his friends had already graduated high school and moved on, and the couple of friends he had who had gone on to the Citadel were already a year ahead of him.

He straightened up and squared his broad shoulders. *Stop it, Gus! One year. It's just one lousy year. Man up! You have no fucking choice. A year behind or not, you'll do this like Dad and Grandpop did.* He inhaled deeply, tried to focus on the clothing spread across the two beds, and started putting his things into duffel bags. *You can do this. You can do this.*

"You *have* to do this," he whispered as he forced item after item into his bags. *At least you sort of know what to expect.*

It all came alive to him when a couple of his senior classmates, guys he was supposed to experience Hell Week with, went on to the Citadel without him. They had filled him in on every shitty detail, and unfortunately they hadn't minced words. Their accounts sounded like his worst nightmares come true. And not only that, now they were also going to be his upperclassmen, giving him shit instead of them getting it all together.

But the grooming had started long before that. Every year from his first birthday on, his father had given him a different book about the Citadel, and as soon as he was able, he'd been expected to read each of them over and over until he'd memorized everything about the institution. In addition, he'd listened to story after story from his father and grandfather about their time at the Citadel—the camaraderie the cadets shared and the feeling of being part of something much bigger than just one man.

Gus had always been expected to follow in the footsteps of his father, and he'd always accepted that he would do it. But attending the Citadel had not been a dream of *his*. At least not at first.

His apprehension wasn't because he didn't think he could handle the exhausting physical expectations or the academic load. The real cause was something Gus had only shared with one other human being. He was gay. He'd known it since he was old enough to know what *gay* meant, and he also knew being gay could never be a part of Citadel life. In fact, it was an unspoken taboo, and he was scared shitless that he wouldn't be able to pull it off.

Being gay and actually *being* gay were two different things to Gus. He decided almost from the day he'd accepted his sexual orientation that he would hide his sexuality in the interest of doing what was expected of him. Thus far, to his credit, he'd succeeded.

But Gus's chest tightened painfully when he thought about what lay ahead of him. He had convinced himself that four years in the closet at the Citadel was really no different from every other day of his life. But now he had the haunting feeling he'd been blowing smoke up his own ass. It *would* be different. How could it not? Until then he hadn't had to share the close confines of a barracks with another male or get naked in the showers or see other guys naked in the shower or, even worse, witness someone jerking off.

Thinking about a fellow cadet jerking off in the shower made his cock stand at attention and his blue jeans tighten uncomfortably. At his age everything made his dick jump. Two seconds of gay porn and he was shooting his load. How in the fuck was he going to get through a shitload of cadets naked in the shower?

Fucking stop it, Gus! He closed his eyes and cursed his weakness again. All he needed was a raging hard-on in the shower to get labeled or, even worse, tossed out on his ass. For the last few weeks, he'd prayed over and over that he'd get a bunkmate who was overweight, unattractive, and had acne and buckteeth. If God took pity on him, maybe—just maybe—he could pull this off.

Suddenly the all too familiar struggle started raging inside of him again. He'd spent years convincing himself he *could* do this. After all, he was tough, and from what he knew, he didn't *look* gay, at least compared to the way the media portrayed gays. But every time he felt a little confidence growing, a small voice sounded off in his head. *Are you really stupid enough to think you can pull this off, that you can actually succeed and not disgrace the family name?* Gus pressed his hand against his churning stomach as his mind continued the ongoing battle. *I have no choice!*

Gus was following in a long line of McRae men. Real men's men. He certainly didn't want to be the one to destroy that lineage. As a small boy, he had gone along with his father's and grandfather's plans without much real understanding of what it meant. Then, when he was fifteen or so, he had discovered the reruns of the old television show *Gomer Pyle, U.S.M.C.* on TV Land. In a weird sort of way, that show gave him some perspective on the military, and after a few episodes, he'd suddenly began to grasp the implications of what his family was asking of him.

The more he watched the show, the more intrigued by the military lifestyle he became. Something about the uniforms and the camaraderie between the men appealed to Gus. He quickly learned the military was a place to belong where things weren't expected of a person based on who his or her parents were. He decided it could be his own place in society, and he wanted to be part of something like that.

He was hooked, but the ugly reality of the situation kept popping back into his mind. *You're gay, Gus.* But if he could keep his sexual identity under wraps, maybe he could make it happen and have a chance at a career in the military. Still, that was a big *if*, and the Citadel was where it was all going to unfold.

Not only was the old television show his first introduction to the military, it was also when he'd developed his first real man crush. Sergeant Carter. The sergeant had given him his first erection right there on the living room couch while chomping on a PB&J. He loved how the guy could be a leader with a tough exterior, but when it came down to it, he really cared for the well-being of his men. He wanted to have a sergeant like that. Hell, he wanted to *be* a sergeant like that one day.

Gus rubbed the back of his neck and squeezed as hard as he could. He hadn't thought about Sergeant Carter in many years, so why now? But as he'd done then, he quickly pushed the thought from his mind. Television was just a fantasy. He was facing the real thing.

In his teenage years, attempting to put his sexuality out of his mind, Gus focused all his energy on his education. He'd fallen in love with history, especially Southern history and particularly the Civil War. He'd taken the ferry out to Fort Sumter so many times he could do the guided tour himself. Since then he'd read every book he could find on the Navy Seals, Delta Force, Green Berets, and Marine Recon, secretly planning his career.

When he gathered the nerve to tell his father his plans, however, the man would hear nothing of it. He wanted his son to graduate the Citadel, yes, but afterward Gus was to get a law degree and eventually join the family legal practice. That became a major bone of contention between them, and after many arguments and heated discussions, Gus had decided to let it alone for the time being. He would go to the Citadel as planned and do the best he could to either prove to his father he would do well in a military career, or convince himself he would not. The proof was in the pudding, and very soon he would see what he was really made of. On the bright side, if he did succeed, by the time he graduated the Citadel, he would be old enough to make his own career decisions, and his father could do little about it.

He was brought back to reality by a pair of soft arms encircling his waist and squeezing. "You seemed really deep in thought," Elizabeth Anne said as she laid her head against Gus's back. "Are you having second thoughts?"

TWO YEARS ago, when Gus had been told he was going to escort a young Elizabeth Anne Ravenel to her junior prom, she'd been described to him as a beautiful, well-bred Southern girl from a fine Charleston family. He'd protested, telling his mother he didn't want to go to the dance with someone he didn't know and that he wouldn't enjoy it. And like most times, he'd lost the battle. But much to his surprise, he *had* enjoyed it.

Elizabeth Anne had been nothing like he'd imagined. She was outgoing, witty, and smart as well as pretty. She'd made him feel at ease from the start and was the kind of person who drew people in everywhere she went. She was sincerely warm and caring, and everyone wanted to be around her. Gus had been exceptionally pleased when, on the way home, she'd informed him he shouldn't expect any physical romance with her. She had long ago decided to save herself for marriage.

That had been music to Gus's ears. He'd never developed the obsession with sex his friends had, and since of course he hadn't been physically attracted to Elizabeth Anne anyway, she seemed the perfect girl for him. Junior prom had led to senior prom and then ultimately to her debutante ball. Gus loved her, but he was certainly not *in* love with her. He hated the lying, but at the time he kept telling himself no one was getting hurt.

But on the evening of her debut, surprisingly enough, the tables had turned decisively. After all the festivities were over, as they walked hand in hand along the battery, Elizabeth Anne had begun to cry. When he'd asked her what was wrong, she didn't answer and cried harder. Once he determined she wasn't sick or in pain, he'd held her until she was able to speak. She said she had been terribly unfair to him. She was so sorry she'd led him on all this time, but they had no future together. And then she blurted out that she was pretty sure she was a lesbian.

Gus remembered the shock he'd felt and then the sense of relief that had washed through him. He'd been feeling guilty for leading *her* on, and now she was the one confessing to what he hadn't had the nerve to tell her. After her sobbing through her apologies, he couldn't allow her to carry the burden alone. He held her by the shoulders and looked into her eyes.

He finally said the words out loud he'd sworn to himself he would never say. "It's okay, Elizabeth Anne. I'm pretty sure I'm... I'm gay!"

Upon hearing his confession, Elizabeth Anne had started to laugh hysterically. He remembered thinking he'd just said the words he never thought he would say, and she was laughing at him. But when he thought about their particular situation, he'd started to laugh as well.

After their mutual admissions, they had spent hours talking about how a marriage between them would be convenient, please their families, and ultimately be a good move for Gus, if he were to join his father's law firm. But they knew they had time before they'd have to make such a serious decision. Besides, Gus still had to get through, or at least attempt to get through, the Citadel so he could see where his path in life would lead him. That evening had sealed their friendship, and whether they were together or separated, she would always be his best and closest friend and confidant.

Gus had been very relieved to have this in the open between them, but he was equally determined to stay in the closet and had sworn her to secrecy. Of course, being the person she was, she'd kept his secret and gone on acting as his beard of sorts. He was going to miss her the most while he was away.

"I'M GOOD," Gus said, closing his eyes and trying to seem strong and assured. "Just thinking about the past and my life for the next four years."

"I hate the thought of you leaving," Elizabeth Anne said. "I can't bear to think about not seeing you every day."

"Me too, Rav," Gus said in a soft tone. He'd started out calling her Elizabeth Anne like everyone else, but that hadn't seemed to fit her. He'd eventually shortened it to Beth Anne and then, over time, shortened it again to Rav, short for Ravenel, her last name. To him that fit her well, and she seemed to like it too.

"I'll have a full schedule at the Citadel," he went on, "and you'll have a full course load at Converse. But remember, Spartanburg is only a few hours away from Charleston. We'll see each other as much as we can. Not as much as we'd like in the beginning, but we'll find a way to make it happen."

She burrowed her face against his back, her arms tightening around him. A small sigh escaped her, and he thought he might have even heard a slight sniffle. He lowered his head and laid his hands over hers. They'd become so close over the last two years, and he truly was going to miss her.

"It'll be all right, you'll see," Gus reassured her.

"Angus, you all packed, boy?" A strong masculine voice said from the doorway.

Angus Conrad McRae walked into Gus's room without knocking or asking permission. Elizabeth immediately dropped her arms from around Gus's waist and wiped at her tear-filled eyes.

Angus seemed to realize he had broken up a tender moment and looked down at the floor, but he didn't retreat. "Oh! Uhh, sorry. It appears I've interrupted something. My apologies to the both of you."

Gus looked at the two stuffed duffel bags, all packed and ready to go. "It's all right, Dad. We were just saying our good-byes. Yeah. I think I'm good to go."

Angus looked up and glanced at Gus's bed. "Well, you better turn in soon, boy. You know your mother is insisting we have an early breakfast with your sister at Hominy Grill before we take you to the Citadel."

"Yes, sir" was all Gus said, but his mind was already working the angles. *Hominy Grill. A place where she's guaranteed to be seen sending her only son off to the Citadel. How typical.*

Angus cleared his throat. "Uh, I'll leave you two to finish your good-byes, then."

"Thank you, Mr. McRae," Elizabeth Anne said. "I'll only be a minute."

Angus nodded and turned to leave the room. He stopped at the door and looked back. "Now, Elizabeth Anne, you know we consider you family, so don't be a stranger around here."

Elizabeth Anne nodded and smiled. Angus left the room, leaving the door open behind him.

Gus felt Rav's hand slip into his. He looked down at her and met her tear-filled eyes. "This is not good-bye," she said, her voice cracking. "This is so long for now."

"I'll call you as soon as I can," Gus promised. "But you know I can't use my cell phone or make any contact with the outside world for the first two weeks."

Elizabeth Anne brushed his cheek with the backs of her fingers. "I remember. And I know you'll call when you can." She went up on her tiptoes and pressed her lips to his cheek in a gentle kiss. "Oh, Gus, I'll miss you so much," she whispered.

He felt his own tears burn at the back of his eyes, but he did his best to hold it together. He really was going to miss her. She'd become such a big part of his life.

When he thought he could talk without losing it, he finally spoke. "I'll miss you too, Rav. It'll just be two weeks. We can manage for two weeks. Right?"

Elizabeth Anne nodded and rested her forehead on Gus's chest. "I need to go," she said softly. With one last press of her lips against Gus's cheek, she turned and fled from the room.

The weight of conflicting emotions pressed down on Gus, overwhelming him until he felt numb. He was scared shitless, sad because he was going to miss Rav, and angry at his mother's transparent attempt to use his entering the Citadel as a notch in her social bedpost. And at this very moment, he felt completely alone. A feeling he knew wasn't going to go away anytime soon.

CHAPTER FOUR
MATRICULATION DAY

GUS LOOKED at the plate of scrambled eggs, grits, and sausage in front of him. His stomach churned, his skin was clammy, and he felt like he was going to throw up. He hadn't slept more than a couple of hours, his mind going over and over the unknown. For all his father, grandfather, and buddies had told him what to expect, it was not like experiencing it for himself.

"Angus! Your mother is talking to you, boy," his father said.

Gus shook his head to try to clear the fog surrounding his brain. "I'm sorry, ma'am. What were you saying?"

Anne-Emerson Beaufort McRae rolled her eyes. "I was saying how proud we are of you." She looked over at Gus's sister, Emerson, who nodded in approval as well. "You're following in the footsteps of your father and your grandfather, and that makes us very proud and happy. And not only to the Citadel, but eventually to join your father's legal practice as well. It's so exciting!"

Oh God, here we go again. I don't need this right now. I wish they would leave it alone. Just this once.

He turned his attention to Emerson and gave her a pleading look. *Please help me, Emmy.* She stared at him with compassion but didn't say a word. So much for his sister changing the subject.

"Angus! Aren't you going to answer your mother?"

He snapped back to reality, and his stomach turned over again. "A lot can happen in four years, Mother," Gus tried to explain as calmly as he could. "I might hate the Citadel and be chomping at the bit for a career in law, but I doubt that very much. I've made it no secret that a life in the military is what I want right now."

"Chomping at the bit, what a lovely expression," his mother drawled with a sniffle.

"That's nonsense, boy," his father chimed in. "We've been over this a thousand times. You've got a partnership in a thriving legal firm waiting for you when you graduate. An opportunity that anyone with a level head would take advantage of."

Gus felt his blood pressure rising. His nerves were frazzled, and he was on the edge of losing it. "I guess I don't have a level head, then" was all he said as he went back to pushing the food around his plate.

His father slammed a fist on the table, causing the water glasses to shudder and almost topple over and drawing a squeal out of Emerson. "You show respect in front of your mother and sister, boy."

"Angus," his mother chided in a low voice. She looked around the small dining room and forced a weak smile, obviously embarrassed by her husband's outburst. Gus watched as his mother laid her hand on his father's forearm. "Everyone is staring, darling. Don't you think this conversation is better suited for the privacy of our own home?"

His father nodded and plastered on the fake carefree expression he reserved for the public as he smoothed the tablecloth in front of him.

Gus took a deep breath in an attempt to settle his stomach. "Just this once can't we have a nice breakfast like everyone else?"

"Darling, we're not like everyone else," his mother said in her haughtiest tone.

Gus simply shook his head in disbelief and then looked down at his watch. "It's time to go, and I'd prefer it if you'd just drop me off, please."

"Drop you off?" his mother whined. "Young man, it wouldn't be proper to drop you off while the other parents go in with their sons. What would people think?"

"Right now, Mother," Gus said, as low as he could but loud enough for her to hear him clearly, "I don't really care what people think. This was my last morning before God knows what, and we couldn't even have a civil breakfast without you both reminding me of my so-called responsibilities and the path you have all laid out for my life. And to be honest, I'm really sick of it."

His mother gasped and put her hand over her mouth in horror. He watched the red creep up his father's face until it looked like his head was going to explode. And to make matters worse, it looked like Emmy was doing her best to keep from smiling.

Gus had taken all he was going to take. He wiped his mouth with his napkin, dropped it in his uneaten plate of food, and stood. "I'll be waiting outside, or if you would prefer, I'll be happy to take a cab."

"You will do nothing of the sort," his father hissed through clenched teeth. "You will wait right here until we're ready to leave as a family."

Gus was getting angrier by the minute. "A family, huh?" he hissed right back. "You mean we're a family as long as I do what you want me to do. That's right, isn't it, D-A-D?"

His mother looked like she was on the verge of tears, and his father coughed to hide his disgust. This time Emerson did smile—until their father glared in her direction and cut her in half with his eyes.

"Shit," Gus mumbled under his breath. *Why do I let them do this to me? And now poor Emmy is going to get the cold shoulder as well.*

His father removed a wad of bills from his wallet and dropped them on the table. He stood and pulled his wife's and daughter's chairs out for them. Without a word, his parents walked past Gus, not meeting his eyes, and headed for the front door. Emerson slipped her arm in his, and together they followed their parents.

THE RIDE to the Citadel was quiet and uncomfortable. Gus was pissed they'd managed to ruin his last morning with their proper Charlestonian airs. He knew from past experience he should have expected something like this, but he'd hoped maybe just this once they could behave like the rest of the world. When they reached the Citadel, his father pulled into the parking lot at Johnson Hagood Stadium and stopped the car. He was about to turn the ignition off when Gus spoke up.

"I was serious about going in alone," he said softly. "Since I'm such a disappointment, it's probably best if I do this on my own."

His mother was now shaking her head and sniffling. She reached into her black suede Prada bag, retrieved a perfectly pressed white linen handkerchief, wiped her nose, and gently dabbed under her eyes.

She turned to her son with a distressed look. "But...."

Gus interrupted her. "Don't worry, Mother," he said calmly. "I'll tell anyone who asks that you couldn't bear to say good-bye to your only son. That should impress your society friends. Right? Poor, poor Anne-Emerson. She just couldn't endure it."

His father whipped around in the seat and glared at him. "Why you ungrateful.... Now you listen here, boy."

Gus patiently waited for the onslaught of insults that normally followed a confrontation like this. He was a fool to turn up his nose at his father's offer to bring him into his firm. He was stubborn and ungrateful. He'd never properly appreciated all they had given him, all the privileges and opportunities he'd had by virtue of being a McRae. Such a disappointment. Blah, blah, blah.

But before his father could say anything, his mother again laid a hand on Angus's forearm and shook her head. "Let's just do as he asks, Angus."

His father glared at him a moment longer. Gus refused to look away or change his expression. He'd be damned if he would allow his father to bully him today. And much to his relief, Angus the elder turned around and placed both hands on the steering wheel without another word. The silence in the car was deafening, but after thirty seconds or so, his father reached down to the side of the seat and popped the trunk of their Mercedes.

Gus hugged Emmy, and she kissed his cheek. "Good luck, big bro. You got this," she whispered and squeezed his hand.

"Thanks, sis," he said with a wink.

Gus turned to his parents in the front seat. They were very stiff and continued to face forward. With a sigh he said, "I'm sorry it always comes to this." He stepped out of the sedan, shut the door behind him, and walked to the rear of the car. Once he'd raised the trunk lid, he reached in and grabbed his backpack and duffel bags and then slammed it shut again. With his head held high, Gus proceeded to the check-in station to find out what battalion and company he would be part of. He waited nervously until he reached the head of the line and handed over his paperwork to a waiting cadet.

Without looking up, the cadet handed his papers back and said, "Fourth Battalion, Company T for Tango. Proceed to the Watts Barracks to meet your TAC Officer."

"Thank—"

"Move along. Next."

As he approached the Hagood Gate, Gus stopped and studied the handsome cadet standing at attention outside the guardhouse, his white-gloved hand positioned across his gray-and-black wool uniformed chest. Gus felt a quick tingling in his groin at the mere sight of the uniform but quickly forced those thoughts from his mind. Instead, he wondered when and if he would ever be assigned to that post.

His mind quickly drifted back to the numerous times he'd been through these very gates. Every Friday afternoon the cadets put on a parade for the general public, and Gus had attended the extravaganza regularly, but something about walking through the gates today felt so totally different. His knees started to tremble, and he realized that if it weren't for the weight of his duffel bags steadying his hands, they would be shaking as badly as his knees. Suddenly he pictured himself in a dramatic scene—collapsing from nerves and landing flat on his back sprawled out on the sidewalk with people stepping over him. That image forced a nervous chuckle out of him, calming him a little. He willed his feet to move once more, and he walked through the gates as a civilian for the last time.

When Gus saw what was happening all around him, it hit him harder than he thought it would. The sight of nervous recruits hugging their teary-eyed parents for the last time before the family was banished from the campus made his heart ache. As much as he loathed what his parents stood for with their social climbing "family values," they were still his parents, and at this particular moment, they would have been better than no parents at all. He felt a brief stab of loneliness mixing in with his nerves, but he kept moving and started talking himself through it. *So what if there's no one to hug you good-bye? You don't need them. You don't need this moment. This is not why you're here.*

Gus sighed as he pushed the feelings to the back of his mind and even forced a little smile when he thought about how he'd denied his parents their high-society show. After only a few more steps, he froze in place like someone else was in control of his feet. A fine sheen of sweat developed and caused his clothes to stick to him as his stomach did backflips.

For the first time in his life, he was truly petrified with fear. He closed his eyes and shook his head in an attempt to dissipate the anxiety that gripped him, but the act did little good. Gus took slow deep breaths. *You can do this. Simply put on that fake smile Mom and Dad taught you and get the job done.* Gus opened his eyes, took one last deep breath, and squared his shoulders. *One step at a time.* It was very difficult to look straight ahead when the campus was so busy with activity, but whoever was now in control of his body had finally decided to propel him forward.

The campus was so familiar, yet it felt as if he were seeing it for the first time. Summerall Field, or the parade deck as it was frequently called, was a massive field in the center of the campus where all the marching parades and much of the PT and weapons training took place. The grass was lush and green, and the field was buzzing with activity. It was all so recognizable from his many visits, but he still couldn't get over the fact of how foreign it seemed. How many times had he seen the row of working cannons and flagpoles flanking the east perimeter? The six-foot-high replica of the Citadel graduates' class ring on the southeast corner and the various military tanks, helicopters, and fighter jets strategically placed on every corner of the field. All well-known, yet he couldn't shake the strange feeling of being on alien soil.

The sight of the other cadets being shown around by their Academic Officer with their parents at their sides caused a lump to form in Gus's throat. He swallowed it down quickly and pushed those thoughts deep into the back of his mind. *You're better off alone in this,* he thought to himself. *If Dad were here he'd know everyone, and you'd surely lose your anonymity. Yep, better off doing this on your own.*

He slowed when he saw a group of cadets in full uniform carrying boxes across the parade deck. The sight of their newly shaved heads glistening in the Charleston sunshine told him they were part of the Corps Squad. He knew they'd arrived a full week ahead of him and already had Hell Week behind them. *They're still standing,* he thought. *I guess it can't be that bad. But man, I wish I had this behind me too.*

From across the parade deck, Gus located the sign for Watts Barracks. It was located directly behind Law Barracks, one row off the parade deck. He stopped again and looked at the massive stone structures he and classmates would call home for at least the next few years. All the barracks were four stories tall with castle-like appendages encircling the top. There were windows spanning the structure on every floor, and each had only one archway as an entrance and exit.

He remembered from his research that the archway was called a sally port, and through each he could see a massive tiled courtyard. There was a flurry of activity in every direction. Vehicles lined up in front of the barracks as parents and cadets unloaded their belongings while other cadets directed the traffic. He couldn't get over how many people were moving about.

Gus sucked in a deep breath and bowed his head. *You're ready for this. Go and claim what's yours.* When Gus exhaled the huge amount of air he'd taken in, he released the nerves keeping him frozen in place. He raised his head and started walking toward his future.

Following the signs Gus traversed the walkway between the Law Barracks and the Padgett-Thomas Barracks until he reached his destination. He huffed out a nervous breath as he walked up to the table outside the sally port. His heart was beating wildly, and for the fifteenth time today, his legs felt like noodles. He dropped his duffel bags at his side and tried to steady himself as he accepted the outstretched hand of a uniformed officer he assumed would be his First Sergeant.

As they shook, the man spoke. "Good Morning, I'm First Sergeant Sean Porter." Gus saw Sergeant Porter studying him for a second. "And you are?" he finally asked.

Oh shit! Gus thought. He fought the urge to slap himself in the forehead and instead accepted the offered hand. "Sorry, sir. I'm Angus McRae, but everyone calls me Gus."

"Welcome to the Citadel, Gus."

First Sergeant Porter released Gus's hand and referred to a list he held in his other hand. He flipped through page after page and finally looked up. "Here you are. It looks like you're assigned to room 5445."

"Thank you, sir."

"Proceed through the sally port and meet your upperclassmen," the First Sergeant instructed.

The Cadre! He knew this part was coming, and he was so dreading it. He'd heard horror stories about the degradation the Cadre bestowed on Knobs. Prepare yourself, Gus.

"Yes, sir," Gus said and turned on his heel. The moment he rounded the corner and entered the tiled courtyard, he was hit in the chest with a wad of clothing and his ears were assaulted with loud yelling. So much mayhem. He dropped his duffel bags by his side and caught the clothing as the Cadre pummeled him over and over again. Uniforms, PT shorts, T-shirts, dress uniforms, and a bathrobe were only some of the things he recognized as they flew through the air in his direction.

"Knob McRae," one of the Cadres yelled, standing so close Gus could feel the guy's spittle on his face.

He swallowed hard and replied. "Yes, sir."

"Why are your uniforms wadded up in your arms?"

Gus thought back to everything he'd read. *Do not encourage them. Damn, what is the correct response? And suddenly it came to him.* "No excuse, sir."

"Good answer, Knob," a second Cadre yelled. "Now gather your things, get to your room, put this crap away, change into your PT uniform, and report back here. Got it?"

Elated that he'd responded correctly, Gus exhaled. "Yes, sir," he responded as he scrambled to make sure nothing had fallen through his arms.

The first Cadre stepped up again. "And you've got less than five minutes to do it. Do you want to know what will happen if you're late?"

"No, sir," Gus yelled, already making a break for his room.

Gus picked up his bags and followed the signs to room 5445. He'd read somewhere that all the Fourth Battalion rooms started with five, but he couldn't remember why. But he did remember that fifty-four in the room number meant Fourth Battalion and fourth floor and the forty-five was the actual room number. So with that knowledge, he made his way up four flights of stairs, followed the signs, and eventually found his room.

He dropped one bag and turned the handle, pushing the door open hesitantly. "Hello?" he asked, not sure if his roommate might have arrived before him. No answer.

Gus pushed the door all the way open and found the room empty. He took a few moments to take in his surroundings. The room was about ten feet wide by eighteen or so feet long with white stucco walls and hardwood floors. There was one set of bunk beds against the wall, a row of lockers, a floor-to-ceiling mirror, and two desks and two chairs.

He dropped his bags and the pile of clothing he was carrying on the floor and took another quick look at his room. *Home for the next nine months.*

Realizing he was quickly running out of time, Gus fumbled through his duffels for his tennis shoes and white socks with one hand while trying to sort out the blue shorts, T-shirt, and neon-yellow belt with the other. He stripped, re-dressed, and looked at himself in the mirror. *A Citadel cadet!*

Quickly glancing at his room on the way out, Gus thought it looked like a hurricane had been through it. He ran back and gathered his things into his arms. *I guess since I'm here first, I get to pick my bunk.* He looked up and threw his things on the top bunk and headed for the door.

The minute the Cadre saw him exit his room, they started yelling up at him from the courtyard. "Come on, Knob, get down here, now! Move it, move it!"

"Are your legs broken, Knob McRae?" he heard another one scream.

"The cadet said now!" yet another Cadre bellowed.

Gus took the steps three at a time, and when he reached the courtyard, he fell in with the other Knobs standing in a single line. As Gus joined the formation, the other cadets, one by one, glanced over at him briefly. Each of their eyes seemed to be filled with the same apprehension and fear of the unknown he was feeling. From out of nowhere, Gus had this overwhelming need to be strong, help ease their fears, and let them know in some way it was all going to be okay. He calmed his racing heart and tried to relax. He flashed a confident smile at each of them, nodded, and even winked at a couple. Was this the camaraderie he so longed to experience?

While in line Gus observed all the parents standing on the sidelines, watching their sons and daughters dressed in their PT uniforms, the fathers seemingly bursting with pride as they consoled their teary-eyed wives. And one quick glance down the line told Gus that his classmates seemed to be standing a little taller as well. Some were smiling a little now, some even quietly chatting with the cadet standing next to them. All appeared to be doing their best to hold it together and not let on that they were scared shitless. Gus thought it was mostly for their parents' sake, but he hoped it was the first sign that they were already starting to come together as Company T.

In the quiet of his mind, Gus watched the parents of his fellow Knobs. Again, it made him feel very alone, and he fought the sadness trying to creep back in. Before he could dwell on his thoughts overmuch, a uniformed officer walked up to the line of Knobs and paraded up and down, giving them the once-over. Gus stood up straight, pushed back the negative feelings fighting for brain time, and listened.

"Welcome to the Citadel. I'm Major Robert Strong, and I'll be your Academic Officer. In a few minutes, I'll be taking you and your family on a tour of the campus to get you familiar with your surroundings."

You and your family? Ha!

"This tour will be very casual," Major Strong continued. "It allows you a little more time with your families and gives you all the opportunity to ask any questions you may have."

The major looked over at the parents and back to the cadets. "Are we ready?"

Everyone nodded, and a few cadets even yelled "Yes, sir" as they fell out of formation.

The group, led by Major Strong, exited Watts Barracks and crossed the street to the parade deck. The major began the tour on the southeast corner of Summerall Field, heading north. They passed four academic halls where various classes took place and then turned to the west with a brief stop at the Daniel Library. Next on the tour was the steps of the Summerall Chapel, where the major explained the religious activities offered to cadets and their families. The tour continued heading west along the parade deck, with the major pointing out the bell tower clock, explaining that the last bell chimes at 2100 hours and that's when all cadets are required to be inside the Citadel gates.

Mark Clark Hall was next. It housed the campus bookstore, the dreaded barbershop, the post office, a small canteen for snacks, and Buyer Auditorium. Continuing on, the group moved past four more academic buildings before stopping at the McAlister Field House, a six thousand seat facility and the home of the Citadel's basketball, volleyball, and wrestling programs, as well as the athletic department's administrative offices.

Turning west, they passed Deas Hall where the major pointed out the indoor pool, racquetball courts, and fitness centers, as well as a fully equipped gym. Heading east again, the last and probably most important stop was Coward Hall, which housed the mess hall where the cadets would have breakfast, lunch, and dinner.

The two-hour tour was finally winding down, and Gus thought it had been very informative. Major Strong had confirmed all the building locations Gus had identified when he'd first arrived, as well as a few others he'd missed. When they arrived back at Watts Barracks, Major Strong told them they had one last stop.

The Academic Officer escorted them to one of the dorm rooms he referred to as the squad room. He explained to everyone that this was where all the cadets met before PT for an inspection to check each other over. When Gus reached the doorway, he stopped and peeked in. Being six feet four inches tall, he could see over almost everyone. The room was full of Knobs from the Corps Squad, checking each other over before inspection, and Gus locked eyes with one particular Knob who was leaning against the wall in the back of the room.

The two cadets held each other's gaze. He was much shorter than Gus, maybe five ten or five eleven, but there was something about the way the guy was looking at him. Gus couldn't tell what it was, but he studied the man intently. The Knob's face was almost pretty, but in a masculine sort of a way. Of course his head was shaved, but what little stubble was left looked dark. The thing that held Gus there, though, was the guy's eyes. Even from a distance and in the limited light, the cadet's intense gaze changed between green and brown and held Gus's attention, mesmerizing him, making him weak in the knees.

Gus grabbed the doorjamb to help steady himself. "Damn, that guy is good-looking," he mumbled. Then he quickly realized he'd said that out loud. *Shit!* He looked around, and luckily the tour had moved on and no one was near him. When he looked back to where the cadet had been standing, he was no longer there. Gus shook his head and started walking to catch up with the others. *Oh hell no, Gus! Don't! Can't go there!*

Everyone was again standing in the Watts Barracks courtyard. Gus was walking along in a daze, still struggling to shake off whatever had happened back in that squad room. He was instructed to one area of the courtyard as the cadets were separated from their families. One by one, the cadets were led up to a table inside the sally port. Another uniformed officer sat behind a long table.

Gus waited in line, and when he reached the table, the officer looked up at him and offered his hand. "I'm Col. Martin Taylor and I'll be your TAC officer. Do you know what TAC Officer means, son?"

Gus accepted the handshake as he nodded. "Yes, sir," Gus replied, still in sort of a daze. "Tactical Officer."

"And you are, son?"

"Sorry, sir. I'm Angus McRae, but everyone calls me Gus."

"Welcome to the Citadel, Gus."

Gus nodded. "Thank you, sir."

"If at any time you have any issues, I'm your man. My job is to guide you through this process and make sure you know exactly what is expected of you. Is that clear?"

"Yes, sir."

"Now say good-bye to your family and get settled in your barracks."

Gus felt another pang of sadness. "My family couldn't be here, sir, so I'll just go up and get settled in."

The colonel looked up, and Gus could have sworn he saw a little pity in the guy's eyes, but he said nothing and only nodded.

THE NEXT few hours Gus lost himself in the mundane tasks of unpacking and organizing his room. As he worked at the mindless chore, he found it odd that he still didn't have a roommate. But since he had an endless list of chores to take care of before he turned in, he didn't have too much time to dwell on it. He mulled over a mental list as he unpacked his linens and started to make his bed. In addition to making his bed, he still had to iron uniforms and polish shoes to get ready for church on Sunday. *Church!* He frowned at that thought. All Knobs were required to attend church every Sunday for at least the first six weeks of the semester.

Gus wasn't much of a religious man, but every Sunday morning his parents had made him and Emerson attend Trinity United Methodist Church in downtown Charleston. "It's family time," his father would preach. "We need to see others and have others see us as a family." Gus smirked thinking about how it was never really about the family or God, but always about the family *image*. He mimicked his father again. *The McRaes are a fine Christian family.* But that couldn't have been further from the truth. Anger mixed with a little sadness attempted to creep back in, but as always, Gus pushed it to the back of his mind.

An hour later he grabbed a quick bite in the mess hall and hurried back to his dorm to finish his chores, eager to be ready for tomorrow. Putting the finishing touches on his shoes, he stifled a yawn and looked at his watch. *Nine thirty.* He carefully placed his glossy spit-shined shoes in the bottom of his locker and studied them, along with his neatly pressed uniforms. He was rather pleased at the way it all came out. He took one last look around his room, satisfied that everything was as it should be. He gathered his shower bag and bathrobe and headed for the latrine.

The latrine was across the hall and three doors down. It was one large room with showerheads lined up against the far wall, sinks built into countertops against the opposite wall, urinals to the left, and toilet stalls to the right. *So much for any privacy*, he thought as he stripped off his clothes and turned on the tap. He waited patiently as the water warmed up and then stepped under the steaming spray. He savored the feeling as the hot water beat down onto his shoulders. It had been a very stressful day, and the pounding water seemed to wash away some of the tension. Halfway through his shower, another classmate entered the bathroom, glanced in his direction, and followed a similar routine to Gus's. Soon they were showering side by side, and Gus found it quite odd to be showering with someone, especially a guy. His high-school gym had had shower stalls with plastic curtains for privacy, but he guessed those days were long gone. The guy nodded, and Gus returned the gesture, but casually turned his back without making eye contact. He finished showering quickly, keeping his eyes lowered, then stepped away, wrapping a towel around his midsection. He knew he had to get used to this drill, but he didn't trust himself just yet.

SUNDAY WENT as expected. Breakfast at seven o'clock, church at eight o'clock, and then three introductory classes starting at nine thirty, each two hours long, on harassment, hazing, and bullying. There was a short lunch break between the first and second class and a thirty-minute break between the second and third class. By the time Gus had finished all three classes and dinner, he was exhausted and running on information overload. But the one underlying theme he got from every class was that the Citadel encouraged camaraderie between the cadets, but not at anyone else's expense, and that message was driven home at every opportunity.

Over the course of the day, Gus had recognized a couple of upperclassmen he'd gone to high school with. He would have said hello, but none of them even as much as acknowledged him. *Pecking order, Gus. Remember the pecking order.* He knew he'd have to make some new friends, but everyone seemed to be on edge and lost in their own heads with the unknowns of Hell Week quickly approaching. Gus got back to his dorm room, hoping that maybe a late arrival had taken up residence, but a quick scan offered no such luck. *You're still on your own, Gus, ole boy. Enjoy it while you can.*

HIS ALARM sounded at five thirty. Gus needed to be up, showered, dressed in his PT uniform, and in the courtyard by six o'clock for the first day of Hell Week, and he certainly didn't want to be late. After a brief formation, his company was informally marched over to McAlister Field House, where they listened to a welcome and pep talk from Commandant Mercado. By the time they exited the building, Gus knew he'd made the right decision in the Citadel. He felt empowered and almost ready to take on the world. Unfortunately, that feeling didn't stay with him for very long.

The minute he pushed through the double doors of Watts, everything went horribly wrong. *The Cadre!* Those angry upperclassmen again. Because he was so tall, they had to stand on tiptoes, but they managed to get their faces just inches from his as they ranted and raved incoherently. They yelled louder and louder and started shoving until his company was maneuvered into a rudimentary formation. The Cadre marched them over to the mess hall for breakfast, yelling the entire time about how pitiful they looked in formation, and led them right to the steps of Coward Hall. There they were instructed to form a single line behind the Cadre and wait.

There was more yelling when each Knob was ordered to walk rapidly to their assigned table, which would be theirs for the entire semester. After finding his seat, Gus stood at attention behind his chair and waited for the other Knobs to fall in behind him. When everyone was at their table, they were ordered to "rest" or to "take seats."

They were then instructed to sit on only the front three inches of the seat of their chairs with their backs straight upright. "Three inches, no more!" the Mess Carver yelled. The Mess Carver was an upperclassman who sat at the head of each table and was responsible for manners and the overall conduct of the table. The meal was served family style, and the upperclassmen were the first to plate their food. Once all the upperclassmen were comfortably seated with their heaping plates of dinner in front of them, the Knobs were then allowed to plate what was left. Gus and the other Knobs did as they were told and again waited.

But instead of giving the order to eat, the Carver started quizzing each of the Knobs. "You," he said, pointing to the guy sitting next to Gus. "What's on the dinner menu?"

Gus knew from everything he'd read that he should restrict his eyes to his mess, but he instinctively glanced briefly to the left, and the cadet looked like the proverbial deer in headlights. *Shit! I shouldn't have done that.*

"Don't know, sir."

"Why not, Knob?"

"No excuse, sir."

Apparently Gus's interest hadn't been missed by the Carver, who pointed at Gus. "If you're so interested, Knob, you tell me, then.

And if you can't, before PT, you're gonna do his twenty push-ups and twenty of your own."

On the way into the mess during all the mayhem, Gus had remembered something his grandfather told him about how he should always memorize the day's menu for all three meals. So he'd taken a quick glance at the bill of fare written on a whiteboard, and it was a damn good thing he had.

"Beef tips over rice with brown gravy, sir!" Gus yelled. "Grilled chicken with vegetables and mashed potatoes and…." *Fuck! What was the last thing? Oh Yeah!* "And broiled trout with french fries and corn on the cob… sir!" The Mess Carver glared at him through squinted eyes, obviously pissed he knew the answers, but then he moved on to the next Knob.

Gus waited until the Carver had finished quizzing the other Knobs on everything from current events to history and had given the order to eat. Unfortunately, one of the cadets picked up his fork a little too soon and the Carver slammed a fist down onto the table, making everything rattle from the force of the blow. His company froze as they were instructed to all drop their forks, place their hands in their laps, and wait. The Carver started eating his meal and raving about how good the food was, making all sorts of yummy sounds. They waited. And waited. And waited. And finally after at least fifteen minutes had passed, they received the order to eat. Gus hesitantly raised his fork, focused only on his mess, and took his first bite. His eggs and bacon were close to ice cold, but it all tasted like heaven.

Breakfast was quick, and before he knew it, Gus was being yelled at again to take his tray to the trash and get back into formation. When his company had complied, they were forced to march in the direction of Mark Clark Hall.

A chill ran up Gus's spine when he realized what was up next. *Shit! You knew this was coming, Gus.* He *had* known it was coming, but somehow he'd tried to block it out of his mind. But that was no longer possible. When his company reached Mark Clark Hall, they were marched up the stairs and joined three existing lines disappearing into the building. The line moved quickly, the clacking sound of the clippers getting louder and louder until it was almost deafening. When Gus rounded the corner, he saw three barbers at the head of the three lines. There were piles of blond, brunet, and red hair surrounding the base of each barber chair. He looked around, and all the cadets' eyes were as big as saucers. Each shaving took no more than forty-five seconds, and then the next person was in the chair.

When it was Gus's turn, he squared his shoulders and bravely climbed into the chair. The barber put a drape around his neck, covering his chest and shoulders, and flipped on the clippers. The noise was ear piercing, and the blade felt hot against the back of his neck and scalp. In the mirror Gus watched as the clippers came up and over the top of his head and the barber shook a load of his dirty blond locks onto his chest and smiled wryly. After six or so passes, Gus's hair was gone, buzzed down to a quarter of an inch. The process was both humiliating and degrading, but Gus tried to tell himself it was all part of making everyone the same. Gus remembered his grandfather's words. *Boy. They'll make you look the same, act the same, eat the same, and be the same. They're gonna break you down to one common denominator before they can start to make a man out of you.*

The Cadre filled the rest of the day with grueling physical training, formation and marching drills, learning the proper way to iron your uniform, polish your shoes, make your bed, and how to live your life the Citadel way. By the time dinner was over and Gus reached his dorm room, he was physically and mentally exhausted. He'd been yelled at, pushed around, mortified, and debased, all in the course of one day. He climbed up, collapsed into his bunk, and fell instantly asleep.

When loud familiar voices filled the echoing hall, Gus sat straight up in his bunk. *What the fuck!* The sound of fists slamming against the walls was getting closer and closer. He looked at his watch and saw that it was ten thirty on the dot, but before the time could register in his brain, his dorm room door flew open and two Cadre stormed into his room. They began by pulling his ironed uniforms out of the closet, throwing them on the floor, and stomping on them. Next they emptied all of his drawers, his underwear and socks flying in every direction.

The Cadre marched back and forth in front of his bunk. "Get up, Knob! This place is a mess. What do you have to say for yourself?"

Gus gritted his teeth and gave the same answer he'd given previously, "No excuse, sir."

"On the floor, Knob! Now! And. Give. Me. Twenty!"

Wearing only his briefs, Gus jumped down from his bunk, landed on the floor with a thud, and gave the Cadre twenty push-ups. When he was finished, he got to his feet and waited for his next set of instructions.

The Cadre got right in his face and hissed, "Now I want five laps around the courtyard."

Gus looked down at his bare feet and glanced at his sneakers under his bed.

"Don't even think about it, Knob. I gave you a direct order. Now! Move!"

Gus hit the door and took the steps three at a time again until he was in the courtyard and making his laps. There were other Knobs scurrying around everywhere, some naked, some half-dressed, and others somewhere in between. After his laps, he returned to his dorm room to the awaiting Cadre.

"You're not done, Knob! Get your toothbrush and follow me."

Again, Gus didn't say anything but gathered his toothbrush and followed the Cadre out of the door. When the upperclassman turned left and crossed the hall, Gus knew what was coming next. The Cadre kicked the latrine door open and headed straight for a stall.

Are you fucking kidding me?

With a smirk, the Cadre simply pushed open the stall door and pointed to the grime, dried piss, and God only knows what else around the base of the toilet. For the first time since his arrival, Gus really wanted to knock that smirk off the Cadre's face, but he knew that would only get him in more trouble. He dropped to his knees without a word and started scrubbing the toilet with his toothbrush. He scrubbed and scrubbed as the Cadre looked on. Eventually the upperclassman kicked the stall door. "That's enough, Knob! Back to your room."

By the time the raid was over, it was after midnight. Gus still had to get his room back in order, iron his uniform again, and make his bed. It was well after one thirty when he collapsed in his bunk for the second time in the same night.

THE NEXT three days were more of the same. Up at five thirty, PT at six, breakfast at seven, then more PT, weapons training, and marching until lunch, then start all over again until dinner. The training was grueling, and the Cadre wasn't much better. Gus was more tired than he could ever remember, but he wasn't broken. It had taken everything he had, and he'd had to dig really deep to get through it all, but he was going to make it.

When Gus's alarm sounded at five thirty, he slapped at it haphazardly until it silenced. He threw the covers off and stretched, and then a slight smile formed on his lips. *It's Friday! Thank God, it's Friday!*

Friday signaled two things. Hell Week was nearly over, and at 1600 hours his company and battalion would attempt their first parade. Family and spectators would not be allowed for the first parade, but the thought of putting all those marching drills to good use was very exciting. He hopped out of bed with renewed energy, taking time to make his bed as he'd been trained. There would be an inspection this morning, and he wanted to be ready. As he dressed in his PT uniform, he realized he was looking forward to his first parade as a Citadel cadet, but more so looking forward to the end of Hell Week. Sure, he would have more PT and drills, but they would now be mixed with classes five days a week and study time. The load of both sometimes seemed overwhelming, but after Hell Week, he figured he could accomplish anything.

That morning was the usual PT, but after lunch they practiced their drills a few more times, then were given time to get into their leave uniforms and assemble in the courtyard of their barracks for further instructions. When Gus's battalion marched through the sally port of the Watts Barracks, he imagined what it would be like next week when the parade deck was loaded with cadets' families, alumni, and other spectators. He couldn't wait to actually hear the cannons blast, one by one, like he had when he'd been here endless times as a spectator. He also imagined the sound of the Citadel marching band, the Regimental Band and Pipes, in addition to the drum corps, all doing their thing, and suddenly, he decided Hell Week hadn't been so bad. The overwhelming sense of being part of the Citadel hit him hard. His pulse was racing, and he focused on steadying his lower lip, which was threatening to quiver with pride. He held himself in check and buried the emotions for another time.

IT WAS finally Sunday, and the last day of Hell Week was here at last. After breakfast the Knobs reported to their battalion for instructions as they'd done after every meal since their arrival and were ordered to be in their leave uniforms and ready to go right after dorm inspection. Gus, as well as all the other Knobs, knew where they were going. It was common knowledge that on the last day of Hell Week, the Knobs were all bussed out to the Citadel beach house on the Isle of Palms. Upon arrival, they would be treated to a barbeque lunch prepared by the Citadel alumni as a sort of congratulations for making it through Hell Week. There was no agenda, and the Knobs were free to move about and do whatever they wanted to do. When Gus's bus arrived, most of his fellow Knobs were asleep, having taken the hour ride to catch up on some much-needed rest, but they regained some of the excitement when the aroma of barbeque hit their noses.

Entering the beach house, Gus scanned the place. Knobs were everywhere. Some were huddled in corners, heads propped against the walls, seemingly fast asleep. Others were tucked away in nooks writing letters, while still others were conversing about the horrors of Hell Week. Most Knobs were hanging out in pairs, most likely roommates, but since Gus still didn't have a roommate, he hadn't really bonded with anyone. The rigors of Hell Week left little time for making friends.

Gus grabbed a plate of food and took a seat on the fireplace hearth. He instinctively sat on the first three inches of the raised hearth, but quickly realized he could relax and even slump if he wanted to. As he ate, his thoughts drifted to Rav. He wondered what she was doing and thought it was time to drop her a short note to let her know he was all right. As soon as he finished eating, he dug through his backpack and withdrew a notepad and a pen. He dropped his head and stared at the blank pad. *Where do I start?* Before he could put pen to paper, something compelled him to look up and scan the room. And there, walking toward the exit and being hurried by another cadet, was the hazel-eyed Knob he'd seen in the squad room during his initial tour. The other cadet stopped when their eyes locked again, ever so briefly, and then just like that, he was gone. Gus really didn't know why, but his heart started racing. He shoved his pen and pad into his backpack and got to his feet as quickly as he could. He started for the door, weaving through the crowd, but by the time he'd made it to the exit, there was no sight of the handsome cadet.

Disappointed and feeling a little stupid, Gus went back to his perch. He finished the letter to Rav and leaned his head against the fireplace to rest for a few minutes. The moment he closed his eyes, his mind was assaulted with images of the hazel-eyed cadet. *What is it with that guy?* He shook his head to clear the thoughts and was startled when a fellow Knob from his company tapped him on the shoulder, signaling it was time to go.

As Gus boarded the bus, the sun was being replaced with low-hanging dark clouds, and it started to rain. He took a seat, rested his head against the window, and closed his eyes. It wasn't long after that the movement of the bus and the sound of the rain lulled him into a deep sleep. In his dreams he again saw the Knob with the greenish-brown eyes. This time the cadet was smiling at him. As they held each other's gaze, it was as if the man's eyes could change colors between green, gold, and brown at will. Even from a distance, the gold flecks in the cadet's eyes made the surrounding green look like dark, rich emeralds. But in his dreams they simply stared at one another. Neither of them moved or spoke, and all the other cadets simply faded away until it was just the two of them gazing at each other and very comfortable doing so.

Gus was rudely awakened by the Guns N' Roses version of "Welcome to the Jungle" blaring outside the bus. He opened his eyes as the vehicle drove through the Hagood Gate. Gus held his backpack in place on his lap to hide the lingering effects of his dream. Through the rain and darkness of the gloomy afternoon, hundreds of upperclassmen were clanging the gates and yelling at them. Gus suddenly felt like he was entering a prison. *They're here!* The other cadets had returned from summer break, and he knew his life was about to get a little more complicated.

When the bus came to a stop, it was quickly surrounded by out of control, dripping wet upperclassmen. Gus decided the best plan of action was to get back to his dorm room as quickly as possible. He thought for some reason he'd be safe there and could avoid all the craziness that was soon to follow. And by the grace of God, somehow he made it. But the moment he reached his floor, he knew he'd counted his blessings too soon. The Knobs in the busses that preceded his, who had the same idea to get to the barracks, were now being pulled out of their dorm rooms half-dressed, forced to their knees, and quizzed on the history of the Citadel. Gus suddenly wished he were invisible. He slipped into his dorm room seemingly unnoticed and leaned his back against the door, breathing heavily. Before he could catch his breath, he could feel the vibration of the pounding fists on his back as the upperclassmen banged on his door.

"Get out here, Knob, now! If I have to come in there and get you, it's going to get much worse."

Gus exhaled, straightened his back, and opened his door. Two of the Cadre were again waiting for him. "On your knees, Knob, with your hands behind your head."

Gus dropped and awaited instructions.

"Who was the first graduate of the Citadel and in what year?"

Holy shit! Gus racked his brain. He knew this. He'd studied this crap day after day for months. *You can do this—just think.*

One. Two. That's it, Twe! "Twe," he yelled. "Charles Twe, sir." Gus had always learned things by association, and this was no different.

"When?" The Cadre screamed into his ear, obviously pissed that he'd known the answer.

Gus panicked. *When? Think, Gus, think!* For the life of him, he couldn't remember. For some reason, 1845 kept popping into his mind. He didn't know why, but since he had no other answer, he went with it. "In 1845, sir."

The moment the date left his mouth, he knew it was wrong. Something about 1845 always popped into his mind, but he used that as a foundation. It was 1846. Just one year later.

"Drop down and give me twenty," the Cadre yelled.

"I meant 1846, sir," Gus answered. "It was 1846."

The Cadre almost smiled. "Get back in your room and don't come out again."

Gus got to his feet. "Yes, sir," he answered, bolting for his door.

Again safely inside the privacy of his room, he leaned against the door. His heart was still pounding, but he'd made it through yet another surprise attack by the Cadre. Gus climbed up and sat on his bunk, listening as the chaos went on right outside his door. It was nearing six o'clock and time to head over to the mess hall for dinner when things finally quieted down. Gus was about to jump down from his bunk and get ready for dinner when his door slowly opened.

He held his breath, thinking the Cadre was coming in for another round, but much to his surprise, he met the hazel eyes of his mysterious, but now soaking wet, cadet.

Chapter Five
From One Hell to Another

THE OLDER guys on the team had warned Sam about the *welcome back* the regular Knobs would receive once they returned from the beach house. However, he had been totally unprepared for the intensity of the mayhem. The dark clouds and torrential rain only added to the bedlam. And the sounds? Dear God, between the claps of thunder, howling wind, and the constant screaming of the out of control Cadre, the noise rivaled the roar at Ford Field, which had always left Sam's ears ringing for days after watching the Lions play. About as much shoving and tackling too. All he wanted to do was hide in his room and sleep, but no. Fucking Greg had up and quit, and now that the Knobs who were not Corps Squad had completed their Hell Week, he was being assigned to a new room. Heaven forbid he had a room to himself and a little privacy until he had time to adjust and get a handle on this insane new life.

Yeah, well, apparently wishes weren't currently being granted.

Dripping wet, his pack on his back and a duffel bag in each hand, Sam pushed his way through the chaos in the congested hallway. He finally found room 5445, shifted his duffels into one hand, and pushed the door open.

Sam's mouth nearly hit the floor.

For some stupid reason, he hadn't expected anyone to be in the room, and he sure as fuck hadn't expected to see wide gray eyes looking back at him. The same eyes attached to the tall, sexy man who'd starred in a few nighttime fantasies of late.

Sam quickly caught himself, looked away, and snapped his mouth shut. He glanced at the numbers on the door, hoping he'd made a mistake, but no such luck.

"This your room?" Sam fought the urge to roll his eyes at the stupid question that popped out of his mouth. The guy was sitting on his bunk; of course it was his room. *Way to go, genius.*

"Yup, and I'm left to assume since you're loaded down, it's now your room too?"

Sam tilted his head. "Loaded down?"

"The bags," tall, broad, and too fucking hot for words responded, nodding in the direction of the duffel bags.

First, Sam needed to stop being so dense and second, broad and tall were both fine adjectives to apply to his roommate, but no more *hot* references. Ever!

"Oh, right," Sam finally squeezed out. He shut the door and pressed his back against it. "Sorry, I'm a little off my game after the craziness out there. I'm Sam."

"Gus. I hope you don't mind I took the top bunk. I feel a little confined down there."

"Sounds reasonable, given your size and all."

Gus smiled, and fuck if that didn't make him all the more handsome. Sam looked away, unable to meet Gus's gaze, irritated with himself and his inability to control his lust. He'd do well not to look at the man at all if he were smart.

"It has its advantages."

"I'm sure it does."

Sam placed his bags on the bottom bunk and quickly assessed the desk situation, but found nothing sitting on either of them. "You claim one of those too?" he asked and waved toward the desks.

"The one on the left, but if you prefer it, I'll be happy to switch."

"No problem." Sam dropped his backpack in the closest chair and tried not to think about how much he liked the Southern lilt of Gus's voice or how the words rolled off his tongue, making him sound refined and proper. Like many of the others who attended the Citadel, Gus was probably rich, pompous, and entitled. He probably had no clue what hardship and hard work meant. It didn't matter how attractive Gus was, more than likely he'd turn out to be an ass. And Sam had no use for asses. Well, at least not attitude wise.

Nope, he wasn't going there.

He was sure as he spent more time with his roommate, Gus would become less appealing. Probably Sam would learn to despise the uppity kid, and with that realization came some measure of relief. Dislike he could deal with.

"Your accent speaks of the Midwest."

"You got a problem with that?" Sam snapped as he emptied the contents of his backpack into the desk drawers.

"No. I was merely making conversation and pointing out the obvious."

"Which is?"

"You're not from around here."

"Detroit."

There, that should put Gus off. Detroit had a bad rep, as did the people who lived there. Some of the hype was well founded, but that didn't mean it wasn't a good place to live or that everyone who lived there was a hoodlum. The thought of Gus looking down his upturned nose at him caused Sam's skin to prickle with irritation.

"Cool. I'm from Charleston."

"Figures," Sam grumbled, still not looking at Gus.

"What's that supposed to mean?" Gus asked, sounding offended.

"Nothing." Sam opened one of the locker doors. It was empty, so he shoved his backpack inside and then grabbed his duffels and dropped them on the floor next to the locker. He opened the bag with his uniforms and shoes and unpacked.

"You're not much of a conversationalist, are you?"

"Nope."

The door flew open, effectively stopping Gus's chatter when two upperclassmen rushed into the room. "What the hell is going on in here? Why is this room such a mess?"

"I was just reassigned to this room and unpacking my things."

"No excuse, sir," Gus announced and jumped off his bunk to stand at attention.

Sam shot Gus an angry glare. He had to tilt his head back to do it. Jesus, the guy was taller than he'd first realized. Sam was no runt at five foot eleven, but where Gus was broad and thick with muscle, Sam was lean, the perfect physique for a running back, and he was fast. His frown deepened. *Ass kisser.*

The second cadet pushed past the one who had asked the questions to stand directly in front of Sam, snapping his attention back to the present problem. *One at a time, Sam.*

"You better take some lessons in manners from your bunkmate. Now drop and give me twenty."

What the hell was going on? Hell week was supposed to be over and the day celebrated. Was this seriously his fate for the next year? Sam gritted his teeth and huffed out a breath. "Yes, sir."

He grudgingly went to the floor and counted off twenty, letting his irritation propel each movement. By the time he was done, he disliked Gus even more.

The feeling was cemented when the first cadet stabbed a finger into Sam's chest. "You just earned yourself latrine duty. Report to the loo at 0500."

"Yes, sir."

The two cadets retreated, slamming the door behind them.

"You'll make it easier on yourself if you answer next time with 'No excuse, sir.'"

"I'll keep that in mind," Sam spat and returned to unpacking his things, shoving them forcefully into the closet, not trying to hide his anger.

"Hey, whoa, I'm not the bad guy here. I've already been on latrine duty, and it sucked. At least he didn't tell you to bring your toothbrush."

Sam caught a glimpse of Gus as he climbed back up onto his bunk, and forced his eyes away. He wasn't going to check out Gus's ass, dammit, and even if the guy sounded sincere, Sam wasn't going to like him. Being in such close quarters with Gus would be way easier if he kept him in the asshole, rich-kid category. Even if Gus wasn't, it was where he was staying. It was a dickish thing to do, but Sam would be damned if he'd jeopardize his schooling and goals because he had the hots for his roommate.

Back home he was out to his friends and family, but here, within the confines of these hallowed walls, he couldn't be. One day, after graduation, he could stand up and proudly state that a gay man not only graduated from the Citadel, but did so with honor and dignity. Maybe then they'd change their views, but not today.

Sam finished putting his stuff away without another word or so much as a glance in Gus's direction. He shoved his duffels beneath his bunk, grabbed his kit, towel, and clean clothes, and headed to the showers to get ready for dinner.

He had to fight his way through the crowded hallway, but it was worth it to be free of Gus. Tomorrow he'd put in a request for a room transfer. He'd already survived Hell Week. He'd be damned if he would be thrown into literal hell.

CHAPTER SIX
WHAT THE HELL?

AS THE door opened and closed behind his new roomie, Gus stared wide-eyed, trying to get a grasp on what the hell had just happened. He smacked himself in the face a couple of times to make sure he hadn't drifted off again. *Ouch!* The sting assured him he wasn't dreaming.

As the realization set in, Gus's confusion quickly morphed to blood-boiling anger. *What the fuck is this guy's problem?*

"He's an arrogant asshole," Gus said aloud. "That's what Sam's problem is."

What the hell did Sam mean by *figures* when he'd learned Gus was from Charleston? He'd had people prejudge him on more than one occasion when they'd found out he was from old-money Charleston, with all the wealth and privilege that implied, but this guy knew absolutely nothing about him. He didn't even know his last name. How could he judge him?

Propping his hands behind his head, Gus stretched out on his top bunk, willing himself to relax. It wouldn't do him any good to stay pissed at the guy. They had to share this tiny space for an entire semester. If the guy was an asshole, he was an asshole. Gus would simply have to live with that. But he also reminded himself it was just a semester—fifteen weeks. Hell, compared to the shit he'd had to deal with throughout his life, it would be a piece of cake. He'd had to make the best of a bad situation for the last twenty years, living with a controlling father and socialite mother. If he could survive that, he certainly could deal with an asshole from Detroit for a semester.

Detroit? He'd never been to the Motor City, but he'd seen enough on the news to know it was a pretty rough place to live. The economy was struggling, and those conditions always produced a lot of crime and poverty.

When the anger started to ebb, it didn't take long for Gus's mind to flood with images of Sam. He quickly thought back to the times he'd locked eyes with the handsome cadet. After each encounter he'd doubted if there had been any connection, had convinced himself he'd imagined the entire thing. But the look on Sam's face when he'd opened the door and their eyes once again met said otherwise. It seemed obvious Sam had experienced something when he first walked in. Could the look have been disgust because Gus had sort of cruised him, or was it something else?

Maybe that's why Sam had acted like such an ass. *Could he be confused and closeted like I am? Or even worse, maybe he's a fucking homophobe?*

Before Gus had time to consider it for too long, the door swung open and a freshly showered Sam appeared, wearing only his pants and a white T-shirt. He was carrying his shoes in one hand, his towel and uniform shirt were flung over his left shoulder, and his dopp kit was stuck under his right arm. Sam's brow glistened from a thin layer of sweat, and Gus couldn't help but wonder if it was from the hot shower or if his nerves were getting the best of him.

Gus remained still as Sam closed the door behind him and slowly turned around. Their eyes locked once again, and Gus defiantly held the gaze until Sam looked away. *Yes! A point for me!*

Silently, Gus tracked Sam's movements as he dropped his stuff on his bunk and retrieved socks from the closet before plopping down in the chair. Gus bit his lip to keep from laughing at the obvious attempt Sam was making to avoid meeting Gus's gaze. He hadn't missed the way Sam kept glancing at him out of the corner of his eye. The pursed lips and deep frown Sam was sporting were even funnier. However, seeing the clean uniform reminded Gus time was running out, and he still had to shower before dinner. He glanced at his watch, and although he was finding perverse pleasure in making Sam uncomfortable, he needed to get a move on. He hopped off his bunk, grabbed his own dopp kit and towel, and stood next to the door. He couldn't resist one last opportunity to pay Sam back for his earlier slight. Gus waited silently until Sam looked up. Only then did Gus walk out with not so much as a single word.

WHEN GUS returned from the shower, Sam was nowhere to be found, nor were there any signs of his belongings. With the exception of a neatly made lower bunk, the tiny room looked exactly like it had before Sam had shown up. For some reason the sight gave Gus a melancholy feeling. Just to reassure himself Sam hadn't packed up his things and fled, he nervously peeked into Sam's locker.

Nope! All of Sam's things were immaculately arranged by type—leave to dress uniforms, hung shirts to slacks. His navy blue PT shorts and T-shirts were carefully folded on the top shelf and his shoes were arranged in the bottom of the locker next to the folded duffel bags and his backpack. *At least he's neat.*

Feeling relieved but not sure why, Gus closed the locker door and sat on the edge of the lower bunk as he had before Sam arrived. Realizing what he'd just done, Gus instantly jumped up and smoothed out the taut bedding that Sam had obviously worked hard to make perfect. *Shit! You're not alone, Gus. Stay off of Sam's bunk.*

Before heading out, Gus checked his uniform in the mirror and then paused at the door. He looked back to make sure nothing was out of place and all of his things were where they needed to be. Sam already made the assumption Gus was a snob; he wasn't about to give him reason to call him a slob too.

Satisfied their room was in order, Gus ran down the stairs, lowered his head, entered the Knob lane, and started his brisk walk. He stopped along the way to acknowledge and salute the Cadre and upperclassmen, which was expected of him, but other than that kept his chin to his chest until he reached his destination. Hell Week might be over, but not much would change, only the intensity and frequency of the crazy. He was still a Knob and would be until the end of the year.

Gus stood in the doorway to the dining hall. It was an odd feeling not to have to sit with his company after marching over and sitting together every meal for a solid week, but odd wasn't bad. At least he had this one night of freedom at the end of Hell Week, and he was going to take advantage of it.

The dining room was fairly busy but calm. A sharp contrast to the hell they'd just been through after returning from the beach. He subconsciously did a scan looking for Sam. He could be the bigger man. Since they'd been constantly encouraged to hang out with their classmates, if he saw Sam and he was alone, Gus would try and make nice and join him. He mentally scolded himself when he remembered Sam ate upstairs with the other members of the Corps Squad. But his eyes still darted from left to right almost like he sensed Sam was in the room.

Gus stopped his scan and froze when he saw Sam. He was sitting with a few other cadets, two of whom Gus recognized as Citadel football players. *I guess Sam has a little freedom today as well.* Gus almost took a step in Sam's direction and then stopped. *Fuck it! He's with his friends. And why should I be the one to have to make nice? He's the asshole.*

Gus scanned the dining room again and picked a table in the opposite corner with a clear view of Sam and his friends. He took a seat at an empty table and watched. The cadets were talking and laughing boisterously, probably about the scene when they returned from the beach, and Gus felt a pang of jealousy. He'd not had a roommate since he arrived, and now that he did, the guy was a real jerk. Besides, he didn't need Gus's friendship; he had his football friends. Then a thought crossed his mind. *Could Sam be here on a football scholarship? That might explain the attitude.*

Gus noodled on this theory while he picked at his food. Well, more like pushed it around on his plate instead of eating it, but he'd lost his appetite. About ten minutes after Gus sat down, Sam and his friends were still talking and laughing like comrades as they took care of their trays. A stronger wave of jealousy surged through Gus, and he hung his head, unable to watch Sam leave. All his own friends were sophomores and had no interest in being seen with a Knob. At least for the time being. Even though he'd been with his platoon every waking minute for the last week, he hadn't bonded with anyone, and seeing Sam with his friends only made the envy intensify.

"Good riddance," Gus mumbled. *Who needs 'em?*

Eventually giving up on his food all together, Gus took his tray to the trash and pushed the uneaten food into the can. He returned to his room. He was certain Sam was still out with his friends, but just in case, he entered quietly, not wanting to make matters worse between them.

Much to his surprise, he found Sam lying in his bunk, the blankets pulled up to his waist. His lean but muscular chest was illuminated by a small reading lamp. Gus blinked a few times until his eyes adjusted to the dim light. It appeared Sam was asleep, or at the very least, his eyes were closed.

Not one to miss a golden opportunity, Gus studied his handsome new roommate. He felt a little like a voyeur, but after their previous encounters, he didn't know when he'd have this chance again.

A stirring of arousal heated Gus as he took in Sam's sleeping form. He was even more attractive than Gus had originally thought. What he could see of Sam's body was in exceptional shape. His smooth chest was chiseled, and the well-defined ridges on his flat stomach were more than a little appealing. It was apparent he spent a lot of time in the gym. Gus frowned. It had taken him a solid year to get back into shape after his accident, to rebuild his strength. He might be larger than Sam, but in his opinion, Sam looked much stronger.

Gus's dick started to fill, and he was about to adjust himself when Sam suddenly opened his eyes. *Shit! I'm so busted.*

Heart racing, dick throbbing, Gus looked away quickly and rushed to his closet, hiding the evidence tenting his pants. *Fuck!* If this got out, he'd be the laughing stock of the barracks. Or worse, people would think he was a total perv.

Completely embarrassed he kept his back to Sam and kicked off his shoes. As he released his belt, he could feel Sam's eyes on him— or maybe it was his paranoia. Either way he didn't dare turn around. Instead he glanced toward the mirror and was totally surprised to see Sam watching him intently. From that angle Sam couldn't see Gus's face, but Gus had a great view of Sam. The expression on the cadet's face was unmistakable. Lust.

Gus smiled, and a thrill raced through him. The tides had turned. He deliberately took his time unfastening his pants and slowly stepped out of them. Without bending his knees, he leaned down, putting his ass on display as he picked up his pants, keeping his muscles flexed. He stood again, and took his time hanging them up. Slow, deliberate movements. He released the buttons on his shirt one by one and then let it slide over his shoulders. He caught it with his right hand and slipped it onto the hanger over his pants.

He continued to sneak peeks at his new bunkmate, and Sam didn't disappoint—he was still watching attentively. Emboldened by his eager audience, Gus swayed slightly as he ran a cloth over his shoes until they were shiny and leisurely bent over to place them in the bottom of his closet. Before standing up, he slipped off his socks and laid them on top of his shoes. He had to stifle the laugh that threatened when he spied Sam swallowing hard and pressing a palm to his groin. Still, he couldn't help but taunt the man further. He seductively pulled his T-shirt over his head, pausing to take an unhurried stretch. He tightened and flexed the muscles of his back and ass and glanced at the mirror one last time. Not only was Sam still watching him, but he also got a clear view of the tented blanket on Sam's bed.

I am such a fucking tease!

Gus looked down. As expected, his own shorts were still tented. He stretched one more time, making sure to flex as much as possible, yawned, and turned. He did nothing to hide his erection, but Sam had obviously anticipated Gus's move because the cadet's eyes were now closed as he pretended to be asleep.

Oh, but Gus wasn't through teasing. He had one more little maneuver up his sleeve. *Try this on for size.*

He stepped up to their bed and stood there with his hands reaching to the top bunk adjusting his sheets. In doing so, he put his erection directly in Sam's view. Gus smiled as he took extra time turning down his bed, arranging his blankets, and fluffing his pillow. When he was certain he'd put on enough of a show, Gus went back to the desk, turned out the lamp, and climbed into his bunk.

"Good night, Sam," Gus said in a satisfied tone.

No response.

He hadn't expected one, but the smile that stretched across Gus's face was gratified as hell.

This might just turn out to be fun after all!

PART TWO

CHAPTER SEVEN
CADET LIFE

IT WAS an agonizing lesson in restraint, but Sam refused to move so much as a single muscle long after Gus climbed into his bunk. He wasn't about to give Gus proof that he was awake, although he had a sneaking suspicion his new roomie had been aware he was being watched. Because seriously, there was no way in hell a man removed his clothes that seductively unless he was doing so for an audience. Sam wished he'd had the strength to turn his back on the show or bury his head beneath his pillow. That would have shown the arrogant bastard he wasn't impressing anyone.

But Sam was weak, and worse, he *had* been impressed. As much as he hated to admit it, Gus had a magnificent body, the kind that deserved to be seen, touched, licked....

Ugh! Stop it!

Disgusted with himself, Sam finally rolled over and pulled the covers up over his head. What the hell had he done to deserve such torment? He had to have pissed someone off—the man upstairs, someone. Being the poor kid from the wrong side of the tracks was hard enough to deal with in a normal environment, but even harder when he was surrounded by the rich and privileged. He knew he'd have to work harder than most to prove he belonged here. So was it too much to ask that he be given a boring, ugly, and completely unappealing roommate?

Apparently so, since Gus was a walking, talking wet dream who just happened to be attracted to him in turn. Sam knew this with every fiber of his being. Through squinted eyes he'd seen how Gus had been staring at him when he thought Sam was asleep, seen the bulge in the man's pants. Worse, he'd had that hard bulge inches from his face before Gus had climbed up to his bunk. Sam should have just leaned up and bit the thing off. That would have ended the striptease. *I'm so fucking doomed.*

Flashes of panic, anger, lust, want, despair—the list of conflicting emotions went on and on, keeping him awake for hours. But at some point, he'd finally fallen into a fitful sleep.

The shrill sound of an alarm caused Sam to jerk upright and, in the next instant, found him lying back down and staring at the bottom of the bunk above him, fighting a throbbing pain.

"Fuck!" Sam hissed, slapping the snooze button on the alarm clock and rubbing his head, feeling for anything that resembled blood. Almost instantly his pain was replaced with anger. His roomie hadn't even peered over the top bunk to make sure he hadn't knocked himself out cold, or even worse, bled to death from a gaping wound.

His first thought was to kick the bottom of Gus's bunk with both feet as hard as he could, sending him flying out of the bed, but he thought better of it. The motherfucker might be gorgeous, but he was still an asshole, and kicking him out of his bed wasn't going to improve that. *I just need to put in for an immediate room transfer. That's all.*

The thought gave Sam a brief sense of salvation, but then it dawned on him. *What reason will I give the Academic Officer? I know. How about this? Mr. TAC Officer, sir, Gus is a living Adonis, and since I'll be jerking off to him every fifteen minutes, I'll be so exhausted I won't be able to play football and therefore won't be able to fulfill my scholarship. So you see, sir, I need a room reassignment.*

Sam smirked at his own sarcastic head talk. At the same time, he was getting angrier by the second as he realized there was no good reason for a reassignment. He was surely doomed. *You're stuck in this fucking situation for the entire semester, Sam, so you better figure out a way to make this work.*

Sam threw back the covers, stood, and stretched, fighting the urge to glance at the top bunk. Deciding to save some time and make up his bunk before he got dressed for PT, Sam pulled the sheet and blanket up as taut as he could and folded it over, tucking it under the mattress. He knelt on the edge of the bed and reached across to do the same to the far side. His arms were stretched and his ass was in the air when he heard a loud thud. He jumped and hit his head again, the back this time. *Not the fucking Cadre again?*

Preparing himself for whatever was coming next, Sam closed his eyes and took a deep breath, ignoring his throbbing headache. Before he could get to his feet, the door opened, and instead of the Cadre, he saw Gus.

What the fuck? Sam quickly backed out of his bunk and straightened. Gus stood in the doorway, already dressed in his PT uniform and dripping wet with sweat. He had a concerned expression on his face. *Why does the fucker always have to look like he stepped out of* GQ *magazine?*

When what Gus was wearing registered, panic filled Sam's brain. He looked at his watch, thinking he'd missed PT altogether. *Five thirty-five.* Luckily he hadn't overslept and still had twenty-five minutes before he had to report. He rubbed his aching head and looked up to the heavens. *Come on, God. Could you not have at least waited until both my feet were firmly on the floor and I wasn't on my knees with my ass up in the air before you let him walk in? If I have any chance of making it through the semester, I need you to work with me just a little bit?*

"Sorry," Gus said, interrupting his thoughts. "I didn't mean to startle you. The door was stuck, and I had to kick it to jar it loose. Did you hit your head?"

"What?" Sam asked.

"Your head? You're rubbing it like it hurts."

Again Sam rolled his eyes at his own stupidity. *You're rubbing your head like a wounded kid! Do you have to sound like a dumbass every time this guy asks you a question?*

Before Sam could answer, Gus made it across the room in two long strides and stood next to him. Sam flinched a little when Gus touched the back of his head, but surprising himself, he didn't pull away.

"Did you bump it? I feel a lump forming. Let me get you some ice."

"No!" Sam protested. "I'll be fine."

"Are you sure? It'll only take a second."

Out of nervousness Sam looked at his watch again.

"You didn't miss PT, by the way," Gus assured him. "I couldn't sleep, so I went for an early run. Ever since my acc—"

Gus stopped midsentence.

Sam wondered what Gus had started to say, but he clearly wasn't going to share anything further.

"Well," Gus continued, "I've been working on my endurance training. That's all."

While he was talking, Gus kept rubbing the back of Sam's head, and damn if the sensation didn't feel great.

"Uh, I'll be fine," Sam said awkwardly, twisting his head away from Gus and walking over to his locker to get his toothbrush and toothpaste. Anything to get away from Gus's gentle caresses. "It's just a little bump."

Sam grabbed his kit and headed to the door, and when he looked back, Gus was studying him oddly. *Is that genuine concern I see in his eyes?*

Gus squinted and this time flashed an unmistakable expression of concern. "What's that on your forehead?" he finally asked.

Sam sighed. *Fuck! I can't catch a break.* He was about to make up some stupid story when the Citadel's Honor Code popped into his head. *No lying, stealing, cheating, or toleration of the same, Sam! Suck it up and take your due.* He cringed, offered a half smile, and told Gus what had happened earlier that morning when the alarm went off.

Sam was totally caught off guard when the expression on Gus's face turned to one of sympathy. "Man, looks like you've had a rough morning already."

Sam frowned. "Yeah, I guess I have. But I'm okay. I gotta go. Sorry."

Opening the door and closing it behind him, Sam was unable to believe what had just gone down. He slapped himself in the forehead out of habit and wished he hadn't. "Ouch," he mumbled when of course his hand landed right on the egg-shaped bump. "You're such a fucking klutz."

Free from Gus's observation, he looked at his forehead in the latrine mirror. It was an egg all right. Not too big, though. About the size of a sparrow's egg, but an obvious egg just the same. He felt the back of his head gingerly, and that knot was a bit bigger. He wished he still had hair to conceal it.

He looked at his reflection for a few more seconds, shook his head in disgust, and eventually loaded his brush with toothpaste and brushed vigorously, trying to work off some frustration.

When Sam got back to the room, Gus had already changed his T-shirt and was sitting at his desk, writing on a notepad.

He glanced up casually a few times while Sam put on his own blue shorts, T-shirt, and sneakers and then fastened the standard neon-yellow belt around his waist. Sam checked himself in the mirror one last time, wishing again he had hair to pull down over his forehead to mask the small egg-like bump that was now front and center.

The silence between them loomed, and Sam wished he could think of something to say. But he didn't know the guy, and everything he thought to say sounded odd or stupid, so he just kept his mouth shut.

Sam walked to the door and opened it. He looked back. "See ya around" was all he could come up with as he left the room.

"ARE YOU fucking kidding me?" Gus said to the empty room. "'See ya around'? What a fucking idiot."

Gus opened his desk drawer, shoved the letter to Rav he'd been writing inside, and slammed the drawer shut so hard the desk shook. He stood and paced, rubbing his hand over his newly shaved head. *Dipshit! There's got to be something motivating this guy to be such an asshole.*

After last night, Gus felt certain he had the upper hand, but he'd shown weakness this morning when he walked into the room, saw Sam rubbing his head, and expressed concern. It didn't help that he was the one who'd caused the injury when he'd kicked the door. But jeez, he couldn't help himself. Sam just looked so damn cute, like a little boy waking up from a nap.

Gus's anger softened a bit. *There are signs of an okay guy in there somewhere.* After all, he hadn't pulled away when Gus had hesitantly put his hand on Sam's head. And then Gus had seen the second bump. And that had really gotten to him. *But you're going to need to keep your distance, Gus. Nothing good can come of this.*

THROUGHOUT PT Gus thought of little else but Sam for the entire hour of strenuous physical activity. Bottom line, the man intrigued him and, at the very least, made for a big distraction. PT was flying by.

During squats, Gus's mind wandered. Why had Sam taken an instant dislike to him? He'd been disliked and judged before, on more than one occasion, but never before by someone who didn't know his name or where he came from. Sam had been different. It seemed from the moment they actually met, the man despised him. But why? And if the guy hated him, why all the seductive exchanges?

Gus was certain, now more than ever, he hadn't imagined their weird connection. And now he wanted—no, needed to know more. So between his twentieth and thirtieth push-up, he decided he was going to get answers. *Camaraderie, Gus.*

After PT, Gus entered the mess hall, paused, and casually scanned the dining room. He spotted Sam at the base of the stairs, starting up to the second floor, where the Corps Squad ate. He wished they didn't have assigned seating, and he could follow him upstairs to say his piece, but that was not to be.

"What's the holdup, Knob?" an upperclassman yelled. "Move it."

Gus straightened his shoulders and walked quickly to his assigned seat. His talk with Sam would have to wait. Maybe Sam would return to their barracks after breakfast for the short break. If he did, Gus would attempt to have a conversation then.

AFTER BREAKFAST, Gus hurried back to the barracks faster than normal. When he entered their room, Sam was seated at his desk. They existed in silence for the next few minutes while Gus busied himself in his closet. By the time Gus got up the courage to attempt a stab at conversation, Sam was headed for the door.

Gus quickly crossed the room, and before Sam could open the door, he put his hand on Sam's forearm. "Please, wait!"

Sam looked down at Gus's hand resting on his arm and then back up until their eyes met. Sam's eyes seemed to change from green to brown at will, and Gus had to force himself to focus on what was happening.

Gus quickly removed his hand and dropped his arms to his sides. "I was hoping we could talk for a few minutes."

Sam released the doorknob, walked over to his desk, and sat down without saying a word.

Gus took a deep breath and tried to find the right words. "Look, I think we got off to a bad start. But what I don't understand is, why? Have I done something to offend you? As far as *I* know, all you really know about me is that I'm from Charleston."

Sam didn't respond right away, and Gus thought maybe he was struggling to find the right words as well. *Not!*

"Look," Sam said, still staring off into space. "I don't really see us being friends. We have nothing in common. I'm from the wrong side of the tracks of Detroit, Michigan, and the only reason I'm even here is because I can catch a football and run. I could barely scrape up enough money to buy the things we're required to bring with us. On the other hand, no doubt you're one of those high-society, rich Charlestonians whose daddy buys him everything his little heart desires, including his way into the Citadel. So there you have it. Can this be over now?"

Ouch! In Gus's mind Sam had coldcocked him and sent him hurtling back a few steps until he hit the wall. He'd heard the "rich kid" rant before. But what he hadn't expected was for the words to actually smart this time. Somehow he'd thought the Citadel would be different.

Gus stood with his mouth gaping open. He'd been caught so completely off guard, he didn't know what to feel. Hurt was the initial emotion, although it quickly morphed into anger. *So much for everyone being equal here!*

"So that's it, huh?" Gus asked through clenched teeth. "You've written me off because of who you think I am and where I'm from? Without even giving me a chance? That's the shallowest and most judgmental thing I've ever heard. But you know what? That's probably par for the course for a guy who's from the wrong side of the tracks. Shoot first and ask questions later."

Gus shook his head. He walked over to the door, stopped, and briefly looked back. "But don't worry your pretty little head about it. I think I've got it now. The sad thing is, you just lost a potential friend."

Gus opened the door, and while he was still in earshot, he heard Sam's voice.

"Who cares?" the cadet said softly.

Gus stepped back into the room and closed the door again. *He didn't just say that!* Gus's chest tightened in anger. He walked over to Sam, who had now turned away.

He leaned over Sam's shoulder and put his lips close to Sam's ear. "I care," he said. "Just for the record, I don't give a fuck where you're from. And also for the record, we don't get to pick our fucking parents—or how much money they make. Fuck you, Sam whatever the hell your last name is." He was almost whispering. "You know, I thought coming to the Citadel would be different. I thought we would all be the same here. No rich kids. No poor kids. I thought I would be part of something bigger, and if and when I was judged, it would be for who I am and what my capabilities are, not who ignorant, insecure people perceive me to be."

Without another word Gus straightened, squared his shoulders, and left the room. He was so angry he was trembling, but he kept his anger under control until he was away from the barracks. *Fuck him! Who does he think he is?*

Chapter Eight
Détente?

AS SOON as the words passed Sam's lips he regretted saying them. *God! You can be such a dick sometimes! But on second thought, it was worth it to get such a rise out of tall, blond, and handsome.*

Sam remembered the tingle from the cadet's warm breath against his ear when he'd leaned in and started letting him have it. It took all the restraint he could round up not to turn his head and cover Gus's ranting lips with his own, if for no other reason than to shut the man up. But who was he kidding. That would have been all pleasure. *How would you have reacted to that, Richie Rich?*

But the moment Gus left the room, remorse set in. Not that he thought he was completely wrong about Gus, but because he could have handled it with a little more finesse. *Finesse, Sam? Really? That's never been your strong suit. And what the fuck anyway? You've got to put these stupid thoughts about Gus out of your head. You're gonna get yourself expelled before you even play your first game. You were seconds away from kissing the guy.*

Not ready to admit his shortcomings yet, Sam decided he needed a little grounding. He decided to write a quick letter to his mother, sister, and brother. *Yeah! That'll help!* He removed a spiral notebook and pen from his backpack and wrote, *Dear Mom, Kory, and Jenny.* He stopped and tapped the pen on the pad a few times, but nothing worthwhile came to him. He tried to force an opening paragraph but was unable to come up with anything real to say. He realized he was stuck somewhere between desire and remorse, and words escaped him, so he finally gave up. *Fuck it! What's done is done.* Lingering a few more minutes to give Gus a head start, Sam tore the paper off the pad, crumpled it, and threw it in the trashcan.

One of the perks of being on the Corps Squad was that they did drills and weapons training separately from the rest of the Knobs. And that was a good thing. Sam figured Gus needed some time to cool down, so he was grateful he wouldn't have to deal with him again until late afternoon when they returned to the barracks. He didn't know what he was going to do or say when they did come together again, which was inevitable, but he'd figure that out later.

Sam had an hour before he needed to be at football practice, but not wanting to chance another encounter with Gus, he headed to the stadium early.

WHEN SAM finally finished football practice, he was worn out. His tired muscles ached and his back felt like a pretzel. Three hours of drills, lunch, and three hours of football practice had almost done him in. As he had hoped, he hadn't run into Gus at dinner, either because he'd skipped dinner completely or eaten quickly and left before Sam arrived. He was sure it was the latter, but it really didn't matter. He was just happy they'd managed to get through the day without another encounter.

After dinner Sam hung with his football buddies until he couldn't keep his eyes open any longer. His only hope was that Gus was already in bed asleep. He was aware he'd have to deal with the guy sooner or later, but as the day progressed, he'd felt worse and worse about what he'd said. He'd marched and stood in formation with all the other cadets at the Oath Ceremony and recited the Citadel Cadet Creed. A line from that creed kept popping into his mind. *Never shall I fail my comrades!*

Have I failed Gus? Did I prejudge him? The answer to those questions kept coming back with a big definite *yes!* At some point during his walk back to the barracks, he finally accepted what he'd known all along. He'd fucked up royally. And yes, he was going to fix it. Just not tonight. He wasn't ready, and besides, he had no idea *how* to fix it. *I just don't want to face this tonight!*

Fingers crossed, he gingerly opened the door, and much to his chagrin, Gus was still in his uniform and sitting at his desk writing on a notepad. Jesus! Once again Sam was reminded of how perfectly hot the man was. *Even pissed off, he's hot. Even without his hair, he's hot.* Gus shifted a little in his chair, and Sam saw a flash when the lamp light reflected off the number four pin attached to his collar representing his freshman, or Knob, status. That brought his attention to the epaulettes on Gus's uniform, which made his shoulders look even broader than they actually were. *Damn!*

Gus looked up, and when their eyes met, his usually cool gray eyes were a dark steel-gray. Sam offered a half smile, wanting to test the waters, but without expression or a single word, Gus placed his pen on his notepad, stood, and left the room.

Sam wasn't surprised by Gus's reaction. He would probably have done the same thing if the roles were reversed. But they weren't. Sam leaned against the back of the door and closed his eyes. *This is all me! Gus didn't break the Cadet Creed in the first two weeks. I did. Congrats, dude. You probably set some kind of record. Maybe if you hadn't been such a douchebag and gave the guy a chance, you might have even been friends. Is all this water under the proverbial bridge? Either way we can't go through the entire semester like this. You're gonna have to man up and apologize to the guy. He may be Richie Rich, but at the very least, you're gonna have to make an attempt to coexist for the rest of the semester.*

Sam walked over to his desk, and without even thinking about what he was doing, he glanced across at Gus's notepad.

> *Dear Rav,*
>
> *How's it going in Sparkle City? I'm sure it's quite a bit different than the Citadel but equally as stressful in its own way. Hell Week was tough, but I survived. Well that's not true. Not only did I survive, I thrived. I think this is the life for me.*
>
> *I didn't have a roommate for the first week, but I finally got one, and boy, what an asshole. He hates me simply because I'm from Charleston and came from a wealthy family. When I came to the Citadel, I thought I was leaving all the stereotyping behind, but I guess that's not how it works in the real world. Even the Citadel. It's going to be tough sharing this small space for an entire semester, but I'm determined to not let it ruin my experience.*
>
> *More later!*
> *Love, Gus*

SAM FELT immediately guilty for reading Gus's note, but their desks were right next to each other, and it was difficult not to see it. And he had left it out there in the open, after all.

"Rav? Who is Rav?" Sam undressed and hung up his uniform. He felt a tinge of jealousy when he realized Gus must have someone special in his life. *Could Rav be a guy? The name sounds like it's from Indian descent.*

He crawled into his bunk and tried to sleep but sleep never came. The words from Gus's note played over and over in his head. *I finally got a roommate, and boy, what an asshole.* After tossing and turning for who knows how long, he finally decided he would apologize the next morning, although he didn't know how yet. He *had* been an asshole, and he would ask forgiveness, grin and bear it, and try to get through the semester. *You can do this, Sam. As Mom always said, "Make it work."*

Minutes later the door opened, and Gus walked in. He undressed, slipped his notepad into his desk drawer, and climbed into his bunk. This time there was no striptease. No flexing. No bending over. Just a guy climbing into his bunk like any other cadet.

I–want–a–striptease–now! Damn it! The demand rang out in Sam's head, but luckily Gus couldn't hear his thoughts. In a fit of frustration, Sam rolled over and closed his eyes. As his vision faded to black, in his mind's eye, Sam once more saw the muscles in Gus's back and shoulders flexing, expanding, and contracting as he moved.

THE NEXT morning Gus was not in his bunk when the alarm went off. Sam stretched, rolled out of bed, grabbed his kit, and headed for the latrine. When he walked in, the place was silent and appeared to be empty. He went into the stall, relieved himself, and suddenly he heard voices and muffled laughter. He flushed and approached the hall leading to the washbasins, stopped short and peered around the corner. Gus was standing in front of the mirror with nothing but a towel tied tightly around his waist. *There are those muscles again.* But what intrigued Sam more was that Gus wasn't alone. He was talking and laughing with a very handsome cadet. Even from across the room, Sam could see that the twinkle was back in Gus's eyes, and when he laughed, his dimples were pronounced and his smile was broad and bright.

Sam studied the good-looking cadet. But something wasn't right. *Wait! That cadet has hair. He's an upperclassman. What the fuck?*

It was virtually unheard of for an upperclassman to associate in a social way with a Knob. It just wasn't done. But here it was right in front of his very eyes. The two talked and laughed like old friends. Sam was instantly envious of the guy's thick wavy dark hair. From the reflection in the mirror, Sam could see the cadet's dark brown eyes and easy smile.

The door opened, and Sam instantly turned around. A cadet walked in and went right into a stall without even looking in his direction. Sam turned his attentions back to Gus and his friend, who were both laughing so hard they were almost bent in half. When they finally stopped laughing, the upperclassman leaned over and whispered something into Gus's ear, and they both burst into laughter all over again. Sam felt a tinge of jealousy and a shitload of paranoia. *Did they see me peeking around the corner watching them?*

Sam stole one last glance at Gus, who seemed to have his laughter under control but was still chatting away and enjoying himself immensely. With that Sam turned and left the latrine.

On the way back to their room, Sam fought the insecurities that continuously plagued him. *The poor kid from the wrong side of the tracks. The kid without a father. The kid that couldn't afford to pay tuition and had to win a football scholarship to get here.*

Suddenly Gus's words came flooding back into his mind. *"I thought coming to the Citadel would be different. I thought we would all be the same here. No rich kids. No poor kids. I thought I would be part of something bigger, and if and when I was judged, it would be for who I am and what my capabilities are, not who ignorant people perceive me to be."*

Fuck! He's right. I'm guilty of doing exactly what I was afraid others would do to me.

SOMEHOW SAM made it through the day. The more the day progressed, the more Sam wanted to apologize to Gus. He ran back to their barracks on several occasions, but Gus was nowhere to be found. After dinner Sam had to report to the stadium locker room to review the video of the day's practice session, but it was no use. He couldn't concentrate.

When Sam finally got back to the barracks, it was almost ten o'clock. He opened the door quietly and turned on the desk lamp. He expected to find Gus asleep in his bunk, but his bunk was still made up. Another pang of jealousy hit him, but he put it quickly out of his mind. He stripped down to his underwear and climbed into bed. Staring up at the bottom of Gus's bunk, he lay there, waiting. After some time had passed, Sam heard the door open and close. In the darkness, he could see the silhouette of Gus's body. He undressed and climbed up into his bunk again without a single word.

A few minutes later, the silence was killing Sam, but he couldn't think of anything to say. Anything that would make sense, anyway. Then he had a thought.

"Morley," he said and waited.

No answer.

"Morley," he said again a little louder.

"Morley what?" Gus said.

"Yesterday you said, 'Fuck you, Sam whatever the hell your last name is.' My last name is Morley. I'm Stewart Adam Morley. Sam for short."

More silence. When Sam was about to give up, he heard Gus's voice, curt and to the point. "What makes you think I give a shit what your name is? I'll be the first one to admit around here names can be dangerous."

"I believe that if you're gonna hate someone, you should at least know their last name," Sam said.

"Well, in that case, my last name is McRae. I'm Angus Conrad McRae the third. Gus for short. There. You can finally put a name to your hatred. Can I go to sleep now?"

Sam had to smile at that response. "Touché," he said. "But we can't go to sleep just yet."

"And why not?"

"Because I haven't apologized."

"No need, Morrrrley," Gus said, dragging out the name. "You made it perfectly clear what you think of entitled rich kids whose daddies buy their way into the Citadel. I'm still that spoiled rich kid. Nothing has changed since breakfast."

Sam was exhausted, and he didn't want to play any more games. "That's not true. Maybe I've changed, and maybe I see things a little more clearly than I did at breakfast."

"Maybe?" Gus asked skeptically.

"Come on, Gus, cut me a little slack. I prejudged you, and I'm sorry."

More silence loomed between them. Sam hoped Gus was at least considering his words.

"You know, Morley," Gus finally said, "I've been judged all my life simply because of my last name. Did you once stop to think that maybe I wanted to join the Citadel so I could be an anonymous cadet just like everyone else? Be broken down to one common denominator and then together as a company and a battalion grow into something bigger than all of us?"

"To be truthful, no," Sam said honestly. "Not until today. And that's my bad because I came here for the same reason."

Sam paused, trying to decide if he was going to take a chance by giving Gus more ammunition or just leave it at that. But before he actually made the decision, the words came flying out like it was someone else speaking.

"I've been judged too," he said quietly. "But for very different reasons. For me it was not having a father like all the other kids. Or for being poor and wearing hand-me-down clothes. Or for working at a deli since I was fourteen years old when all my friends were out playing so I could help my mom support my brother and sister."

Sam paused, waiting for Gus's response, but none came.

Again, as if someone else had taken control of his mouth, words continued to flow like a rushing river. "It wasn't until a coach at my middle school saw me running from a bunch of senior bullies and realized I was lightning fast that things changed. The coach stuck a football in my hands, and I haven't stopped running since. That's when my life started to turn around for the better. Suddenly the bullies left me alone. I took my skills to high school, where eventually a scout for the Citadel saw me and offered me a scholarship. But I turned it down."

"Why?" Gus asked without hesitating.

"To be completely truthful, my family," Sam said. "My mother was already working two jobs. I was giving her everything I made from my part-time job, and we were still barely making ends meet. I had work, school, and football, and at the time I couldn't desert my family like my dad and stepdad did. Besides, I was insecure and unsure of myself. Still am. And hell, I'd never even left the state of Michigan. How could I venture so far away? So I took the coward's way out and signed up for community college. During that first year, I read every book on the Citadel I could find in the public library. I studied their website and read every alumni blog, and over the course of the year, I matured. My mom got a new job, and the family was doing better, so I decided to take a chance. I contacted the scout and told him I was ready if the opportunity was still on the table. A week later they offered me a full scholarship. It was the only way I was ever getting into a good school like the Citadel, where I have a chance at actually being the man I want to be. Unlike you I had no one special in my life other than my family. So here I am."

"I guess we're not that different after all," Gus said sarcastically. "Wait! What do you mean *someone special?*"

"Rav," Sam said hesitantly.

"You read my letter?"

"I'm sorry. It was right there on the desk, and I couldn't help it."

"Jesus!" Gus said.

Sam's voice softened. "I know. You have every right to be upset. I regretted it immediately afterward, but at the time I just couldn't help myself. I was trying to figure out who you really are."

"Whadaya mean *who I really am?*" Gus asked. "I'm just like you. Just like every other cadet. I want to be a better man. Get an education and graduate from the Citadel."

Gus's academic aspirations were not at all what Sam had in mind. He really wanted to know more about Gus's personal life. His sexual preference, to be exact, but of course he didn't correct Gus.

"You're right. We do have that in common," Sam agreed.

"So did invading my privacy give you any more insight into *who I really am?*" Gus mocked.

"No, but it reinforced who I really am, and I don't like me right now one bit. However, the jury is still out on you, but… I promise, no more judging you or anyone else. And I'm really sorry I went off on you yesterday. I was completely out of line."

"Yes, you were," Gus said, still sounding pissed off.

"You have every right to be upset with me, and I'm sorry."

Gus sighed. "First of all, I don't need your permission to feel whatever I want to feel, and second, I *am* still pissed. But... I'll get over it. Apology accepted."

"Thank you," Sam said, feeling relieved.

A long silence loomed between them. Sam fought the urge to speak, but lost. "Can I ask who Rav is?"

"Nope!" Gus answered. "Good night, Sam."

Apparently he wasn't going to get any more information tonight. "Night," he replied. "And thanks for letting me off the hook."

No response. Sam rolled over, punched at his pillow, and stared at the blank wall. He felt better after getting that off his chest, but he still wondered about Rav. Was Rav someone special but not a girlfriend? *Maybe a boyfriend?* Or was Rav a girl but not a girlfriend? Sam's brain was so tired he closed his eyes and was out almost midthought.

CHAPTER NINE
NURSEMAID

"MOVE IT, Knobs!" the drill sergeant yelled at the top of his lungs. "What are you? Citadel cadets? Or a bunch of old ladies?"

Gus picked up the speed of his jumping jacks and, as a diversion, thought of Sam. Over the last few days, they had sort of started making their way. They weren't best friends, but they were at least civil—maybe even a little more than that.

On the morning before Sam had made his attempt at an apology, Gus had seen him in the latrine. Gus had been talking to Jason Dollason, an upperclassman Gus had gone to high school with. Jason had been Gus's first high-school crush, and they'd been pretty good friends back then. And even though Gus had seen Jason around a couple of times, he knew the upperclassman's dilemma about interacting with a Knob and how that would look, so he'd not made an attempt to approach the guy. But sometimes the Citadel had a weird way of reconnecting people through a common goal and then cementing friendships for life.

And this was one of those times. Gus was hurrying to the bookstore to pick up a required read and an upperclassman was on the sidewalk, his face buried in his own book. Gus removed his hat, asked permission to pass, as was customary, and when the cadet looked up, it was Jason. The two had exchanged a few quiet words and in the process realized they were in the same barracks.

They'd run into one another that morning in the latrine quite by accident and happened to be alone, so they had hung out for a few minutes without the benefit of prying eyes. Except Sam's, that was.

It had been great for Gus to reconnect with Jason and feel a little of the comforts of his old life. The two had been laughing and cutting up about Hell Week and how high school was a piece of cake compared to the Citadel when, much to his surprise, Gus had caught a glimpse of Sam's reflection in the mirror peering at them.

Sam had had a weird expression on his face that Gus thought looked like disappointment. But what could Sam be disappointed about? Was it because Gus was interacting with an upperclassman? Then a thought hit him. Maybe it was because Jason was so good-looking? Going solely on a hunch, Gus had used that opportunity to really ham it up with Jason, and Jason seemed to fall right into his show, not knowing he was actually part of Gus's plan.

Later that night, for whatever reason, Sam had apologized. But truth be told, they didn't actually see that much of each other. Academically they shared several classes. Gus was majoring in Pre-Law to please his father, but with a minor in Leadership Studies to satisfy his desires. Sam was majoring in Leadership Studies and minoring in Business Administration because he already had credits from his year in community college back in Detroit.

But on the Knob front, because Sam was part of the Corps Squad, he didn't have to deal with the PT the other Knobs had to endure. After Hell Week, the Corps Squad didn't do PT with the rest of the Knobs. They didn't do much PT at all unless it was during their sport practice. They got to eat upstairs in the game room instead of the mess hall, and they didn't have to sit on three inches of their chair and be quizzed constantly about Citadel history, the day's menu, or current events. They did literally nothing but go to class and practice their sport. In fact, when their sport was in season, they didn't even have to do Friday parades.

After thinking about the Corps Squad and how privileged they were, Gus thought about how Sam had called *him* privileged in the beginning, and that pissed him off. He certainly wasn't the privileged one now. But being pissed at Sam was a good thing at present. It allowed Gus to focus on something other than the grueling exercises he was being forced to endure at the moment. But he smiled a little when he thought of Sam in another way as well. Those intense hazel eyes and that lean, cut body.

Since they'd sort of called a truce, Gus had started seeing Sam as he had when they first crossed paths on matriculation day. Sure, Sam was rough around the edges, but little by little his sense of humor had started to come out, and Gus learned that Sam was actually smart and funny as hell. When the cadet laughed, his entire face lit up.

Additionally, there was no doubt Sam was a handsome man. But Gus had done a pretty good job of keeping those sorts of thoughts at bay, except at times when he needed an escape. Times like these, and the dark and restless hours of the night when he needed a quiet release.

Luckily Sam was a sound sleeper, and Gus was a quiet masturbator, so it all seemed to work out. On the other hand, Gus was a very light sleeper, and when Sam needed the same kind of release, Gus had been right there with him. On more than one occasion, their bunk had swayed ever so slightly, and Gus had taken advantage of the moment and joined in, imagining Sam's callused hand sliding up and down his long, thick length—something Gus had only witnessed once when they'd happened to be in the shower together. Sam's only sign of an orgasm was a slight increase in his breaths as he shot his load, and Gus would usually follow seconds later, biting his lip as he milked himself dry.

Gus shook his head to clear the memory and adjusted his crotch as he rounded the track for the third time. The Charleston heat and humidity was finally getting the best of him, and his body was covered in sweat, completely soaking his PT uniform. But for once he was grateful for the sweat, which he hoped masked the wet spot he'd caused in the groin area thinking about Sam. When PT was finally over and he was hurrying to breakfast, his chin against his chest, he again thought of Sam. Not in the sexual manner of earlier but in the pissed-off sort of way that had preceded it. It just wasn't fair that Sam, as a chosen one, didn't have to endure any of this PT crap. *I'll remember to give him a shitload of grief for it when I see him!*

Later that night when Gus crawled into bed and tried to quiet his brain, he quickly realized the day had actually flown by. Besides the normal activities, they'd had their first round of racquetball intramurals against Company C in Deas Hall. Gus was an avid racquetball player and had kicked some serious ass. No one had said anything, but by the looks on their faces, the upperclassmen had been impressed. All in all it had been a fairly good day.

Tomorrow was finally Friday. After Parade Drills, all the Knobs, including the Corps Squad, would finally be able to leave the campus for the first time since the trip to the beach house after Hell Week. And after Sunday they'd all be able to use their cell phones again, which would make life feel a little more normal.

The day before matriculation day, he and Rav had made plans for her to come back from Converse for the weekend and attend the parade, and then they would have dinner at Fleet Landing. But of course his parents had insisted on joining them at the parade, along with Emmy, if for no other reason than to make sure they were all seen doing the proper thing. And then to top it off, they had demanded he and Rav join them at Husk for dinner. Not wanting to spend his first night off campus with his parents in a stuffy restaurant, he'd refused, and the compromise had been they would all eat at Fleet Landing. Knobs were not allowed to drink, of course, but simply being off campus would make a big difference in their morale. And seeing Emmy and Rav would be like chicken soup for his soul.

While Gus was lying there, he decided since Sam had no family here, he might take a chance and ask Sam to join them tomorrow night. He probably already had plans with his football buddies, but it would show a little goodwill to invite him anyway.

Just before the toll of the bell, Sam pushed the door open and slipped inside. Gus was still awake, and he rose up on one elbow and rested his head in his hand. "Hey."

"Hey," Sam said back.

"You're in later than usual."

"Yeah, we have our first game in a little over a week against Davidson, and the coach is working us pretty hard. Okay if I turn on a light?"

"Sure."

When Sam turned on the light, Gus saw Sam was cradling his stomach, and he looked extremely pale. "Are you okay?" he asked with genuine concern.

"I'm feeling sick to my stomach," Sam said. "I guess the coach pushed us a little too hard."

Gus watched as Sam stripped down to his underwear and sat on the end of the bunk.

"Maybe you should go over to the infirmary and they can give you something for the nausea."

"Nah," Sam said. "I'm sure it'll pa—"

Before Sam finished his sentence, he bolted for the door.

Gus jumped off his bunk and landed soundly on his feet. He slipped his shorts on and tore after Sam. When he opened the door to the latrine, he heard Sam inside a stall. The poor guy was heaving so violently it sounded like he was upchucking everything inside his body. Between the sound of Sam heaving and his flushing the tankless toilet every few seconds, the noise was echoing off the walls. Gus ran back to their room, grabbed a hand towel, and again hit the latrine. He ran cold water over the towel, wrung it out, and slowly pushed open the stall door. Sam was on his knees, holding on to the rim of the toilet for dear life, his head buried deep inside the bowl. By now there was nothing left but dry heaves, and Sam seemed to be finally empty. Gus laid the cool wet towel on Sam's neck, and he flinched.

He looked up with a surprised expression on his face. "Shit! Get out of here, Gus. You don't need to see this!"

"Shut up, Sam. You're a fellow cadet, and you're sick. We took an oath to help one another, remember?"

"Forget the fucking oath. You're officially off the hook," Sam said between dry heaves.

"Okay," Gus said. "Forget the oath. But you're still my friend, and I'm not going anywhere until I know you're okay."

Sam sighed and shifted so he was sitting on his ass and leaning back against the stall wall. Gus knelt next to him, removed the towel, and wiped the sweat from Sam's forehead. "Do you feel better?"

"I can't tell yet."

"That was pretty serious," Gus said. "If you want, I'll walk over to the infirmary with you."

"Nope," Sam said rather curtly.

"Why not?"

"Because I just pushed myself too hard. It'll pass."

"Sam, that little episode wasn't from overdoing a workout."

Gus laid his hand on Sam's forehead. Even though he'd just removed the cool cloth, he could still feel the clammy heat emanating there. Gus instantly knew Sam was running a fever.

"Sam, you're burning up," he said, again replacing his hand with the cool towel. "You need to go to the infirmary. This is surely some sort of virus."

"No!" Sam said. "I'll be fine. Besides they won't give me anything. It just needs to run its course."

"Fine," Gus said, knowing when to give up on a lost cause. "Do you think you can make it back to our room?"

"Yeah."

Gus stood and offered his hand to Sam. Sam looked at it for a second and then accepted it. Gus pulled Sam to his feet, and Sam instantly fell back to his knees, his head once more in the toilet bowl. He heaved several more times until he was empty again.

"Maybe I should stay here for a little while."

Gus put the towel back on Sam's neck. "I think that's probably a good idea. I'll be right back."

A few minutes later, Gus returned with two Advil and a cold ginger ale from the vending machine. He popped the top, poured it over a cup of ice, and handed the cup and the Advil to Sam.

"Can you sip this? Don't want to get dehydrated."

Sam hesitantly accepted the cup. He looked like he was having trouble even thinking about putting anything in his stomach, but he took it anyway. "I need to lie down," Sam said.

"Here or in our dorm?" Gus asked.

"Dorm," Sam said.

Gus again offered his hand and helped Sam to his feet. Sam was a little wobbly, but he stood on his own. Gus held the stall door open, and Sam gingerly passed through. Gus moved to the latrine door and did the same until they were slowly making their way down the hall. Gus stayed close, and it was a good thing because as they approached their dorm room, Sam's legs gave out, and Gus caught him just before he hit the floor. He slipped Sam's arm around his neck and grabbed Sam's hand. Gus then put his arm around Sam's waist and carried his weight until he got him into their room. When he finally got Sam down in his bunk, Gus straightened and stretched his back. *Damn! That guy's solid muscle.*

Almost as soon as Sam stretched out on his bunk, Gus saw him start to shiver. He pulled the covers up over Sam and tucked them in around him.

"So cold," Sam said, his body trembling and his teeth visibly chattering.

Gus reached up and removed the sheet and blanket from his bunk and spread them out on top of Sam. He pulled his desk chair up next to the bunk and sat down. The cup of ginger ale was on the nightstand, and Gus wished like hell he had a straw. He lifted the cup to Sam's mouth and told him to at least take a small sip.

Sam raised his head enough for his lips to touch the cup, and Gus lifted it just a little until Sam wet his lips and swallowed. Sam lay back down but within minutes rose up to his elbows.

"Oh shit!" he yelled.

Knowing what was coming, Gus spun around and grabbed the trashcan from beside his desk. He held it in front of Sam.

Sam heaved desperately, but the only thing that came up was two Advil tablets and a small amount of clear liquid, which Gus figured was the ginger ale. When the heaves were over, Sam dropped back down. He appeared to be trembling even more.

"Shit!" Gus mumbled. "Are you still cold?"

"Freezing," Sam hissed between clenched teeth.

Gus looked around for anything he could spread over Sam, but there was nothing. They each had one regulation blanket and one set of sheets.

A thought entered Gus's mind, but he quickly dismissed it.

He sat there and watched his friend shivering uncontrollably for a while and finally said, "Fuck it!"

He climbed into Sam's bunk and lay on top of him, covering the guy with his own body.

Sam's eyes widened briefly, but he seemed too sick to protest and eventually closed his eyes.

WHEN SAM awoke sometime before daybreak, he thought maybe he felt the slightest bit better. His stomach had at least settled, and his fever had broken. As he lay there in a warm cocoon of blankets and Gus, the uncomfortable sensation of wet sheets beneath him, he didn't move a muscle for fear of waking the man who was still stretched out on top of him. Gus's face was buried in the crook of Sam's neck, and he was snoring lightly. Sam could feel Gus's warm, steady breaths as each one brushed against the top of his shoulder. He liked having Gus on top of him.

Last night, that move had completely taken him off guard. He'd thought about protesting, but he was too sick. And besides, he had pictured Gus on top of him on more than one occasion. Not this way, of course, but at that point he hadn't cared.

The events of the night before popped back into his mind—all the things Gus had done for him. Following him into the latrine while he hurled his guts up, the cool towel, the ginger ale, giving up his own sheets and blanket, and then climbing on top of Sam to warm him. If he'd doubted Gus's integrity before, he certainly couldn't doubt it now. Not only had he misjudged the man, he'd misjudged him miserably. Gus was an upstanding guy, and he truly believed in the oath and Cadet Creed he'd taken before Hell Week.

Sam savored the weight of the big man on top of him. He closed his eyes and imagined his legs wrapped around Gus's waist and Gus sliding in and out of him, ever so slowly. It had been quite a while since Sam had been with anyone, and he knew it would be that way at least until the school year ended and he went back to Detroit for the summer. But damn this felt good. Especially since it was Gus.

From the first time he'd locked eyes with Gus, he'd experienced this ridiculous love/hate dichotomy regarding the tall, handsome cadet. Part of it was self-preservation. He knew that. But part of it came from his own insecurities and sheer stupidity. No more.

Sam decided right then he was going to make every attempt to build a solid friendship with Gus, if Gus would have him. *I don't care whether he's straight or gay, he's a good guy, and I want him in my life either way.*

Gus stirred a little, interrupting Sam's thoughts. Gus slid off Sam and to his left side. He brought his long leg, bent at the knee, up over Sam's groin and rested it there. He draped his arm over Sam's chest and snuggled against him, but as far as Sam could tell, he didn't wake.

A combination of thinking about Gus and the weight of Gus's leg resting on his groin was causing Sam to grow hard, and the last thing he wanted was for Gus to wake and feel Sam's erection under his leg.

Sam had the urge to giggle like a silly schoolgirl, but he stifled the impulse. Instead his lips morphed into a smile as he slid his arms out from under the covers and wrapped them around Gus. Erection or no erection, he was going to enjoy this rare moment. He closed his eyes, and before he knew it, he was asleep again.

GUS STIRRED at the sound of the alarm clock. He instinctively reached over and slapped the snooze, and the alarm silenced immediately. He settled back against Sam and closed his eyes again. Then he suddenly opened them. *What the fuck!* Sam's arms were around him, and he was snuggled up against the man, his leg thrown over Sam's midsection, Sam's erection obvious under his knee.

Jesus, Gus! What have you done? Then it came back to him. Sam. Sick. Freezing cold. And the rest started to fall into place.

Sam tightened his grip, but he didn't move or speak. Gus had never slept with a man except for his childhood buddies at sleepovers, and he'd certainly never cuddled with any of them. The sensation was odd but also comforting. Sam's strong arms around him made him feel safe, and he was surprised at how much he liked the feeling.

Sam thrust his hips up ever so slightly and pressed his erection into the weight of Gus's leg. Gus froze, fighting his initial reaction to pull his leg away. But he quickly decided he liked how it felt. He'd seen Sam in the shower once, but he'd been soft then. This time Sam was fully erect, and there was no denying he was well endowed. For a split second, Gus thought about moving his leg up and down slowly to see what kind of a reaction he could get out of Sam, but then he thought better of it. He hated he didn't have the courage. He might never again get this chance, but then he remembered having anyone in your bed at the Citadel was grounds for immediate expulsion.

Gus fought the urge to lay his head back down on Sam's chest, snuggle up against him, and just stay there until he figured out what was happening to him, but he knew they both needed to get up. He needed to report to PT, and hopefully Sam would go to the infirmary and get a release to take the day off. But one never knew with Sam.

Forcing himself up on one elbow, Gus broke the grip Sam had on him. Sam opened his eyes and stared up at Gus for a few seconds, looking as disoriented as Gus had been when he first woke up. Gus tried to read beyond the disorientation and pick up on anything going on behind those rich green eyes, but he had no luck.

Not knowing what else to say, Gus hesitantly attempted to speak. "How're you feeling?" His voice came out shaky and low.

Sam didn't answer right away, like he was thinking about the question. "Better I think," he finally said.

Gus slowly slid his leg off Sam—neither mentioning the morning wood—climbed out of bed, and stood looking down at Sam. "I hope you'll go to the infirmary this morning and get permission to take the day off. I think you really need to rest."

"No can do," Sam said. "But luckily we have practice reviews in the locker room today and then class, so I can take it easy some."

"Well. I guess that's something," Gus said.

"Gus?" Sam said.

"Yeah?"

"Thank you for being there for me last night. I won't forget it."

"You're welcome. I know you would have done the same for me."

Truth be told, Gus didn't know that, but he would have to give Sam the benefit of the doubt. For now.

"Hey," Gus said nervously, fighting the urge to bounce from foot to foot. "This is sort of weird, I know, but...." He paused and almost backed out, but Sam was looking up at him with those deep green eyes like he was hanging on every one of Gus's words. "And I don't know if you'll be up to it or not. And besides, I'm sure you already have plans with your football buddies for our first night off campus, but...." Gus stopped again.

"What's up with you?" Sam asked. "Why are you acting so strange?"

"Okay, fine," Gus said. "If you don't have plans, tonight after the parade, my parents, sister, and best friend are all going to dinner. I'd really like it if you would join us."

Sam didn't respond right away, but he didn't break eye contact.

"Never mind," Gus blurted out. "I'm sure you have plans."

"I'd love to," Sam said.

"Wait, what?"

"I'd love to," Sam repeated.

Surprised, Gus smiled. "Great. I'll fill you in on the details later. I've got to get to PT."

Moving through the hall, almost as if walking on air, Gus ran to the latrine, came back, and dressed in two minutes flat. "I'll see you later."

Gus made his way to the door and stopped. He turned around. "I hope you feel better."

"Thanks," Sam said. "Have a great day."

Sam stayed in bed a few more minutes, replaying the events of last night and this morning.

When the alarm had gone off earlier and the big guy had snuggled against him, Sam had taken the opportunity to tighten his grip, and Gus hadn't protested. Even when Sam had pushed his erection up into Gus's leg, Gus hadn't moved. That told him more than a love note to someone named Rav could.

He now knew Gus was either gay or, at the very least, bi-curious, and he was determined to figure out which. And fast.

CHAPTER TEN
DRESSED TO THRILL

IT WAS bright and sunny that Friday morning, and Sam was in the Knob lane, hurrying from breakfast to his first class at Jenkins Hall. So far he'd been able to keep down a scrambled egg, a piece of dry toast, and a little coffee, and considering how violently ill he'd been the night before, he felt pretty good about that.

His first class was one he shared with Gus, and he didn't know if the slight queasiness in his stomach was left over from the night before or because he was a little nervous, anticipating his and Gus's first encounter since last night. Sam had never felt butterflies in his stomach over any guy before, so he was almost certain it was just a weak stomach.

Approaching the doorway hesitantly, Sam saw Gus in his usual seat at the back of the classroom, looking through his textbook. Gus immediately glanced up as if he felt Sam's presence. Their eyes locked, and Gus flashed a smile that lit up the entire classroom. Sam normally sat across the room, but today his legs carried him right to the seat next to Gus.

"Hey," Gus said. "How're you feeling?"

"Pretty good. Considering," Sam said, taking his seat. He leaned in a little. "Thanks again for being there."

Gus smiled once more, and those dimples were front and center. "Happy to do it. I'm just glad you weren't alone. It sucks to be alone and sick, especially when you're away from home."

"Thanks to you I didn't have to be alone," Sam replied coquettishly. *Jesus, Sam! Stop this mushy talk. You sound like a girl.* "But I guess this *is* our home. For now, anyway," he added. *There! That was okay.*

"Good point," Gus said. "Hey, speaking of home. About tonight."

Sam felt a quick tinge of something that felt a little like disappointment. *Is he gonna retract his offer?* "What about tonight?" he said hesitantly, sitting up in his chair, his curiosity now piqued.

"I'm not sure how to say this so it doesn't sound as horrible as it is, but just remember we don't get to pick our parents."

"I know that," Sam said.

"Okay, well…. My parents," Gus said. "Well. Let's just say they are everything you thought you hated about me and my privileged upbringing."

Sam looked away quickly. *Ouch!* That stung a little, but he figured he deserved it. He would let Gus have this one. But he didn't really know how to respond. After he'd been such an ass to Gus, he hadn't given any more thought to the whole wealth and privilege thing. But now, tonight, he was going to have to face it head-on by meeting Gus's family.

Gus must have picked up on Sam's hesitancy. He reached over and put his hand on Sam's forearm. "Please don't back out," he said. "I promise I'll protect you. And… I'll make sure they behave themselves."

The guy looked pitiful, and Sam couldn't disappoint him. "I can take care of myself," he said. "I'm from Detroit. Remember?"

Gus's entire face lit up again as he flashed that million-dollar smile. At that moment Sam realized he would do or say anything to make that happen again and again. *God! You're turning into such a pansy.*

"Don't worry," Sam said. "I'm not backing out. What are we doing, by the way?"

"We're going to the historic Fleet Landing."

"Oh, yeah. A couple guys on the team were talking about that place."

"It's a pretty cool place. It was once the Cooper River Ferry Terminal. In 1940 a hurricane struck Charleston and wiped out the terminal. The US Navy bought the pier, constructed a building, and used it for offloading sailors, loading supplies, and general maintenance. Somewhere around 1970, the Navy retired the use of the building, and it now houses the restaurant. The food's not great, but the atmosphere and the views of Fort Sumter and Patriots Point are incredible. And it's a fun place."

"Sounds good to me. Hell, I'm looking so forward to getting out of here, I'd clean mule shit from behind every buggy in town just to get off campus."

Gus smiled again, and Sam's heart fluttered. But before Gus could respond, Colonel Ekrem called the cadets to order.

Throughout the class Sam cast little glances in Gus's direction, and Gus was always diligently following along in his textbook or had his eyes locked on the professor as he lectured. Gus's profile was almost as perfect as it gets. His nose was appropriately shaped for his face, and his cheekbones were chiseled in a very masculine sort of way. Even the guy's ears were perfect. *Damn it, Sam! How can you go from hating the guy to crushing on him in less than a week?*

Eventually the class ended. "Great class, huh?" Gus said.

"Yeah. Great," Sam agreed, not having paid the least bit of attention to the professor.

Gus shoved his book and spiral notebook into his backpack and stood. "So if I don't see you before the Spirit Run, I'll meet you back at the barracks right after. Okay?"

"I'll be there," Sam said, standing.

"Okay, then." Gus hesitated just a little. "I… ah guess I'll see ya around."

Sam nodded, and Gus walked out of the classroom.

Sam shoved his unopened textbook into his backpack and flung it over his shoulder. *You better get it together, Sam. And get it together quickly.*

EUPHORIA! IT was the only way Gus could describe the way he was feeling. He floated to his next class, not even caring that his neck hurt from pressing his chin so tightly against his chest. And if he were being honest with himself, it had everything to do with Stewart Adam Morley. Gus couldn't help but smile at the sound of his name as it played over and over in his head. Stewart Adam Morley. Stewart Adam Morley. *Angus McRae, I do believe you're having your first man crush.*

Gus's next two classes and lunch went by in the blink of an eye. While in the mess hall, in between answering the standard questions and dutifully entertaining his upperclassmen, he nonchalantly kept an eye on the stairs, hoping to catch a glimpse of Sam either coming or going, but no such luck.

Before Gus knew it, he was outfitted in his Full Dress Salt & Pepper uniform and heading down to the quadrangle to join formation with his company and battalion, waiting for their turn to march through the sally port. The drum corps were doing their thing, the bagpipers were warming up, and the Citadel flags were flying high. The air felt electric with all the energy. The Watts Barracks quadrangle was packed with cadets as far as the eye could see, and Gus was right smack dab in the middle of it all. He was finally a real cadet.

The first cannon exploded, sending a stream of smoke into the air and signaling the First Battalion to march through the sally port, across the street, and onto Summerall Field. At the sound of the next cannon, the next battalion started marching. At the sound of the fourth cannon, Gus's battalion received orders to march. When he cleared the sally port, without turning his head or breaking protocol, Gus spotted Rav and Emmy standing on the street outside Watts Barracks, cheering them on, and his lip did a little quiver, but he held back the tears of pride that threatened to escape his eyes.

In every direction, battalions were crossing the street and barracks by barracks a sea of cadets descended and came together on Summerall Field like they'd been doing this all of their lives. When the last cannon sounded, the Padgett-Thomas Barracks came to life as the Regimental Band entered the sally port and started playing "Citadel, All Hail," the school's alma mater. Chill bumps started at the tip of Gus's toes and worked their way up his body until his scalp tingled with excitement. *I can't believe I'm actually a cadet!* Gus thought about Sam practicing football at the stadium. He must be able to hear the cannons, band, and bagpipes. *I wish he could be here to experience this firsthand!*

As Gus marched in step with his battalion, he thought about how he'd made it through the fears of Hell Week relatively unscathed. He'd risen above the intimidation of the Cadre and also made it through orientation for his classes, as well as the constant ribbing from the upperclassmen in the mess hall and beyond. For the first time since he arrived, he finally allowed himself to think he was actually going to make it there. And make it all the way to graduation.

As his battalion passed the parade deck, Gus straightened, lifted his head a little higher, and wondered if his parents were looking for him. If they were, he wanted them to see how well he fit in here and how much he wanted a career in the military. Whatever doubts he'd had about his future when he'd arrived at the Citadel were now long gone. Whether it was a conscious decision or subconscious one, he knew his father's law practice was no longer an option for him. Now he just needed to find a way to tell them.

AFTER THE Spirit Run, Gus made a beeline back to Watts Barracks. He took the stairs two at a time until he reached their dorm room. Still on an adrenaline high from the parade and the special PT, Gus shoved the door, harder than he'd planned, and it flew open with a thud. Sam was standing there in his Summer Leave uniform with a surprised look on his face and his hat in hand.

"Oh... sorry," Gus said, locking eyes with Sam. "I didn't mean to shove the door so hard. I guess I don't know my own strength," he added with a weak smile, unsure of what else to say.

Sam looked so incredible in his uniform, Gus couldn't look away.

"Am I wearing something wrong?" Sam asked as he allowed Gus to study him.

"No, why?" Gus asked.

"You're staring at me like my fly's open or something."

Gus instinctively dropped his gaze down to Sam's crotch and back up again to meet Sam's eyes.

"Nope," Gus said. "Fly's not down."

"So what, then?"

"Nothing is wrong or out of place," Gus said. "In fact, you look great in uniform."

Sam turned back to the mirror and struck a pose. "I do look pretty hot, if I do say so myself."

Gus tried to stifle a chuckle, but he was unsuccessful.

"What?" Sam asked. "Am I lying?"

"Jeez, Sam, I didn't know you were so vain."

Sam appeared to be doing his best to hold back a smile. He smoothed the front of his uniform. "I mean... look at me. Again! Am I lying?"

"No, Sam. You're not lying."

"Thank you. Now are you gonna stand there and suck in my hotness all evening, or are you gonna get showered and changed so we can go?"

"Oh, right!" Gus said, kicking off his sneakers and peeling off his sweaty socks. The entire time he undressed, he rambled excitedly about what Sam had missed.

When he was down to his PT shorts, Gus grabbed his dopp kit and a towel. "I'll just need twenty."

"Well, make it snappy, soldier."

"Yes, sir," Gus yelled, opening their door and rushing to the latrine.

SAM WAS sitting at his desk when Gus returned, dirty PT shorts and underwear tucked under one arm and his toiletries bag under the other. Gus's towel was wrapped tightly around his V-shaped waist, and the lingering sweat from the latrine was glistening off his farmer's—or should he say PT—tanned body. Sam bit his upper lip to keep from moaning. He stared for a few seconds, mesmerized by the entire vision, and then tried to think of something clever to say.

"Move it, pretty boy" was the best he could come up with. "Time's a wasting."

"Yes, sir!" Gus replied with a salute.

Sam smirked. "You're a funny guy. Now shut up and get dressed."

Turning around in his chair, Sam fiddled around with the things on his desk. In the mirror, he caught of glimpse of Gus as he dropped his towel and lifted one leg to step into his clean underwear. The man's ass looked like he had muscles of steel. The cadet even had little dimples in each asscheek. For a second Sam wondered how those muscles would feel in his hands as Gus plowed into him, but then he shook the image from his mind. *Stop it, Sam! No good can come from this. You've got four more years here, and sex is not part of the curriculum.*

Forcing himself to look away, Sam distracted himself by thinking about the evening ahead. Their first time off campus for a decent meal in two weeks. But he had a lot of apprehension about meeting Gus's family. Gus had warned him, but being warned was very different from actually experiencing it. The only bright side was that he was hopefully going to find out who this mysterious Rav was. *Not that it really matters*, Sam reminded himself. *I'm just curious.*

Sam jumped when Gus laid a hand on his shoulder. "Sorry, I didn't mean to startle you. I'm ready when you are."

Sam looked up at Gus and attempted to swallow the lump that quickly formed in his throat. He'd always had a thing for a man or men in uniform, but Gus.... *Oh my God!* The man's height, broad shoulders, and slim waist filled out his uniform like it was a tailor-made second skin. In Sam's mind, Gus was what he'd always imagined a real soldier looked like. *Hell! The guy could very well be the next poster boy for the Citadel.*

"What?" Gus asked with concern on his handsome face. "Did I suddenly grow a third eye?"

Sam chuckled. "Uh. Nothing," he mumbled, suddenly uncomfortable. "It's just your uniform.... It fits you so well. After joking earlier about how hot I looked in mine and then seeing the way your uniform fits you, I feel like mine hangs off of me."

"Stand up and let me get a look," Gus said.

Sam felt like an idiot, but stood. Gus studied him for a few seconds. He put his left hand to his chin and spun the index finger of his right hand in the air making a turning motion. "Now turn around."

Sam smirked, but he turned around once and stopped.

"Nope," Gus said.

Sam frowned. "That bad, huh?"

"What are you talking about? I meant *nope*, your uniform does not hang off of you. As a matter of fact, I think you wear it exceptionally well."

"Ya think?" Sam glanced at himself again in the mirror.

"Absolutely," Gus repeated. "You totally pass *my* inspection."

"Then let's get this show on the road," Sam said, pressing his hands down the front of his uniform.

CHAPTER ELEVEN
REVELATIONS

TOGETHER THEY walked side by side through the sally port, and Sam was totally caught off guard when a young girl ran up to Gus and threw herself into his arms, nearly knocking him to the ground.

The girl squealed with delight as Gus spun her small frame around and then lowered her to her feet. "My God, you've grown," Gus said with a broad smile.

"Guuus," she whined. "I have not grown. I'm almost sixteen. I think I'm through growing."

"Nonsense," Gus said. "If I say you've grown, then you've grown."

Sam cleared his throat.

"Oh, Sam, sorry. Meet my baby sister, Emerson McRae. Emmy, this is my roommate, Sam."

Sam extended his hand. "Good to meet you, Emmy," he said.

Emmy accepted Sam's hand and gave him a dainty handshake in return. "Likewise," she said, batting her eyelashes and smiling coquettishly.

"Stop it, you little tease," Gus said. "She's always been a big flirt."

"Why, I have no idea what you mean, sir," Emmy said to Gus in a strong Southern accent. "I was just being friendly. Right, Sam?" she added with a wink.

"Absolutely," Sam said. "And I'd expect nothing less from a smart refined Southern belle from such a prominent Charleston family."

"Oh crap," Emmy said, turning to Gus. "He knows about that, huh?"

"Yep! He figured it out the very first day we met," Gus said, winking at Sam.

"He's right on at least one of those counts," Emmy said. "I am pretty smart."

Gus chuckled. "And modest too."

Sam was about to protest when a gorgeous blonde in a short skirt and high heels walked up and stood in front of Gus.

Gus tilted his head, smiled at her warmly, and opened his arms.

"I've missed you so much," she said, launching herself into his embrace.

Gus whispered something into her ear Sam couldn't hear, but she broke into a huge smile.

Stepping back, Gus took the girl's hands in his and held them out in front of him. "Let me get a look at you."

The attractive blonde took a small step back, and her smile was beaming.

"You look radiant," Gus said. "Converse certainly agrees with you."

"I can say the same about the Citadel," she said. "Military life agrees with you too. You look incredible, Gus."

Emmy looked over at Sam and rolled her eyes. "Gross, huh?"

Sam cleared his throat as he offered a weak smile.

"Oh, sorry again," Gus said. "Elizabeth Anne Ravenel, meet my friend and roommate Stewart Morley."

Sam offered his hand. "Very nice to meet you, Elizabeth."

Unlike Emmy's, Elizabeth's handshake was firm and strong. "Oh, please call me Beth Anne. It's nice to meet you as well."

Elizabeth Anne Ravenel? Rav-e-nel. Could this be Rav?

"Sam," Sam said.

"Excuse me?" Beth Anne questioned.

"Everyone calls me Sam."

"Oh. Sam it is, then."

A black Mercedes pulled up to the curb and blew the horn. Everyone turned, and Gus saw his mother waving.

"We better get a move on," Emmy said. "You know how Dad gets."

Sam was still stunned after meeting Rav, but his wheels were turning, and he was trying to think of a way to get out of this situation. The last thing he needed was to spend the evening with the guy he was crushing on, the guy's girlfriend, and the guy's family. When he saw the sedan, he thought he might have his out.

"It doesn't look like there's enough room in the car, so why don't I just hang back and you guys can go and enjoy a nice family dinner?"

"Noooo!" Gus said, his tone one of obvious disappointment. "Sam, I really want you to be there."

Why? To flaunt your girlfriend in my face?

"Come on, Sam," Emmy pleaded. "Please come. I hate always being the odd girl out. We can squeeze. Beth Anne can sit on Gus's lap. It'll be fine."

The expression on Gus's face had now changed to one of anticipation. Gus put a hand on Sam's shoulder and squeezed. "Please come. It would mean a lot to me," he said, his voice full of sincerity.

Shit! The guy's killing me here.

"Okay, if you think there's enough room."

Gus sighed and smiled with obvious relief. "Of course there's enough room."

"Yaaay!" Emmy said, taking Sam by the hand and leading him to the awaiting car with Beth Anne and Gus following.

As they approached the car, an older gentleman Sam assumed was Gus's father got out of the car and walked around, opened the passenger side door, and offered his hand to a woman. She got out of the car, and they stood side by side.

So these are Gus's parents. To Sam, they both looked like caricatures, not real people. Gus's father was about six feet tall, but he was pudgy, carrying an extra thirty or forty pounds. His hair was silver, parted on the side, and long enough to curl up on the edges. He was wearing a pair of khaki slacks, a white shirt, blue blazer with big gold buttons, and a big blue-striped bowtie.

The only way Sam could describe Gus's mother was to compare her to an old department store mannequin he'd seen when he was little that had scared the shit out of him. Like the mannequin, her skin was flawless. Her hair was flawless. Her makeup was flawless, and she was dressed flawlessly. She was even posed like the old mannequin with one hand on her hip.

Gus walked up to his parents. His father stuck out his hand. "You're looking well, Angus."

"Thank you, sir," Gus said.

His mother held out both of her hands, and Gus took them. He kissed her left cheek and then her right. "Oh, Angus," she said. "You look thin and pale."

Sam didn't think he'd heard right. *Pale? He's tanner than I am.*

"Mother, Father," Gus said, gesturing to Sam. "I'd like you to meet my friend and roommate Stewart Morley. He goes by Sam. Sam, meet Angus and Anne-Emerson McRae."

Mr. McRae offered his hand, and Sam accepted it, noticing the firm grip. "Pleased to meet you, Stewart."

"Likewise, sir."

Sam turned to Mrs. McRae. "My pleasure, ma'am."

"Stewart," Mrs. McRae said. "I surely hope you don't regret rooming with my son. He can be a bit messy. Our maid used to complain about his room all the time."

Feeling a little sorry for Gus, Sam took the opportunity to sing his praises. "Not at all, ma'am. He is very neat. As a matter of fact, much neater than I am. And we're very compatible."

"Oh, wonderful," Mrs. McRae said, looking a little disappointed.

"Shall we go?" Mr. McRae asked. "Our reservation is at seven."

Everyone piled into the car, and as Emmy had predicted, Beth Anne sat on Gus's lap. Sam kept glancing at one of Gus's hands resting on Beth Anne's waist and the other on her thigh.

There was no constant chatter in the car like when Sam and his family ventured out on special occasions to the LongHorn Steakhouse or someplace similar, so Sam had time to think.

Gus has a girlfriend. Did my gaydar fail me? It couldn't have. The exchanges? The striptease? The snuggling? Could he have been so arrogant and comfortable in his sexuality that he was simply doing all that because he knew I was watching?

Before Sam had any real answers, the car pulled into a parking lot and stopped. *Just get through the night, Sam. No! Not just the night. You've got to get through the semester. Gus is apparently not gay. Man up and stop crushing like a silly schoolgirl.*

Everyone got out of the car and walked up the steps to the restaurant's entrance. Mrs. McRae stopped.

"Angus," Mr. McRae said, "escort your mother into the restaurant."

Gus removed his cover—the name cadets used for their hats following the Navy's example—and tucked it under his arm. As instructed, he stepped up and offered his arm. Mrs. McRae slipped her arm through Gus's, straightened, and Mr. McRae opened the door. As Gus and his mother walked in, Sam, feeling badly for Emerson and Beth Anne, removed his cover and held it in front of him as he offered both of his arms. They gladly accepted and followed Gus and his mother. When they were shown to their table, the entire party waited as Gus's mother stopped on multiple occasions to greet acquaintances, apparently to make sure she was seen with their son in his Citadel uniform.

Sam observed other cadets eating with their families and wished like hell *his* family was here instead of having to spend the evening with the fucking Vanderbilts.

When they finally reached the table, Mr. McRae pulled out a seat for his wife, stood behind the seat next to her, and instructed Emerson to sit on his other side. Then Sam, Gus, and Beth Anne. Sam was about to take his seat when he observed Gus and his father standing behind their chairs, apparently waiting until all the ladies were seated, and he followed their lead.

Mr. and Mrs. McRae ordered drinks while the rest of the table settled on iced tea or water. Everyone was silent as they studied the menu. *Jesus! By this time my family would be chatting it up, deciding what we were going to order and what we would share.* But there was none of that here.

After everyone had finally ordered, Beth Anne asked Gus to escort her to the bathroom. *WTF? He's gonna leave me here with these people? Can't Southern women go anywhere alone?*

Gus and Mr. McRae both stood as Beth Anne pushed her chair away from the table, and Sam again followed their lead.

With no menu to bury his head in after sitting again, Sam looked around the restaurant. Mr. McRae cleared his throat. "So, Stewart," he said. "Where are you from?"

"I prefer Sam, sir. And I'm from Michigan."

"How did you end up at the Citadel, son?"

"I'm part of the Corps Squad, on a football scholarship."

"I see," Mr. McRae said. "And your people?"

"They're back in Detroit."

"What do they do?" Mrs. McRae asked.

"My mother is an office manager at a local electrical supply company."

"And your father?" Mr. McRae asked.

"To be honest, I have no idea. He abandoned us when I was six years old."

"Oh, that's terrible," Mrs. McRae said. "I'm so sorry."

"I'm not," Sam said. "He was abusive to my mother as well as my little brother and sister... and me. It was tough on my mother, but we made out okay. She worked three jobs and... went back to school. I helped out by working part-time and taking care of my siblings."

"You must miss your family terribly," Mrs. McRae said. "I mean, being in a strange town and not knowing anyone must be difficult."

"At times it is tough, and I do miss my family. But I have friends here. I have Gus and friends on the football team as well."

"Well, I declare," Mrs. McRae said. "Angus! I think we should adopt Stewart and be his host family this year. The poor boy deserves a nice family in Charleston."

Poor boy? Oh hell no! Sam looked around frantically. *Where in the hell is Gus?* He caught Emmy's eye, and she flashed a sympathetic expression.

"Thank you, ma'am," Sam said. "But you don't have to do—"

"I think that's a fine idea," Mr. McRae said, interrupting Sam. "We'll speak to Elizabeth Anne about it when she returns. I do believe the Ravenels were a host family last year."

It appeared to Sam that he had no say in the matter, and they were going to continue to talk about him like he wasn't even there. Gus had warned him his parents could be high-handed. And what the hell was taking Gus so long anyway? Sam made an effort to remain calm.

Then, much to his surprise, Mr. McRae turned to him. "What do you think about the idea, Stewart?"

Think, Sam! How do I decline without offending them? Fucking Gus! I can't believe he left me here to fend for myself!

"I think it's a very generous offer, sir," Sam finally said. "But I have such a tight schedule with football and academics, I don't think I'll have time to even leave the campus."

"Nonsense!" Mr. McRae said. "As I'm sure Angus told you, I, as well as my father, are graduates of the Citadel, and we know some pretty influential people there. I'll see if I can get you a little downtime."

"No, sir! Please! I'm not complaining. I like my schedule. It keeps me very busy, and I really don't want any special treatment."

"Jesus!" Mr. McRae said. "What is it with these young people today, Anne-Emerson? They never want a helping hand."

Emmy interrupted. "Daddy, will you excuse me? I need to use the ladies' room." She turned to Sam. "Would you please escort me, Sam?"

Thank God!

"It would be my pleasure," Sam said, pushing his chair away from the table and pulling out Emmy's.

"HE LIKES you. And yes—he's gay," Rav said, standing in the hallway outside the restroom. "I can see it in the way he looks at you. And... the way he wanted to claw my eyes out when I hugged you."

Gus smiled. "You don't know that. I mean, we've had a few interesting exchanges, but that doesn't mean he's gay. I mean... I'm really attracted to him." Gus caught himself. "Jesus, Rav! What am I saying? It doesn't matter if he's gay or not. We're at the Citadel, and being gay is off limits and grounds for expulsion."

"Oh come on, Gus! You won't be spending every waking minute on campus. You do get leave time. Right?"

Gus nodded. "A little."

"So be model cadets on campus and boyfriends off campus. It's that simple. The fact that you're roommates could get a little complicated, but the way I see it, it's just the icing on the cake. Does your door have a lock?"

"Stop it, Rav. You make it all sound so simple. And no. No locks."

"That sucks, but it is that simple."

"No! It's not," Gus said. "Rav, I'm scared to death. I've never been attracted to a guy before. I mean, I have, but not one I was actually with all the time. One minute I want to beat the hell out of him; the next I want to throw him up against a wall, stick my tongue down his throat, and make out like teenagers. Then the next I'm sick to my stomach just thinking about all of it. It's like my emotions go from one extreme to the other."

"Man! You've got it bad. But what are you so upset about? Kissing him or having sex with him?"

"Shhhh," Gus whispered, putting his finger over Rav's lips and looking around nervously to make sure no one was listening to their conversation. "Both!"

"You're gonna have to get over that," Beth Anne said.

"Oh, so two weeks at Converse and you're some big expert on sex?"

"Maybe," she replied, looking down at the floor and turning a few shades of red.

"Oh my God, Rav. You've had sex with a girl?"

"Her name's Valerie, and she's so cool. Gus, we are so much alike it's crazy. We met in one of my classes, and she asked me out the same day. We've been dating for the last two weeks, and well... two nights ago we finally had sex."

Gus smiled and took her hands in his. "And...?"

"It was magnificent, Gus. I'm learning so much. She's such a patient teacher, and you'll never guess what they call lesbians like us."

"What?"

"Lipstick lesbians," she replied. "Because we're both girly, and we like makeup, dresses, and high heels."

"Seriously?"

"I know. Right?"

"I guess it makes sense," Gus said, shaking his head.

"But enough about me," Rav said. "Sam is adorable, and you need to make a move."

"What? No! I can't!"

"Do you like the guy, Gus?"

"Yeah."

"Then, yes, you can."

"THERE YOU are!"

Beth Anne and Gus both turned when they heard Emmy's voice.

"Thanks for abandoning us, you guys. Poor Sam," Emmy said.

Sam was standing right behind Emmy, and he didn't look very happy.

"Oh no," Gus said. "I'm so sorry. We didn't mean to stay gone so long. We just started talking and catching up, and, well... time just slipped away. What happened?"

"Mom and Dad want to adopt 'poor Sam,' as they call him, as a host cadet for the school year."

That means he'll get to come home with me, and we can spend some time together away from the Citadel. Gus looked at Beth Anne. She smiled, and he felt his lips curl into a smile as well. *She's thinking exactly what I'm thinking.*

Gus then turned to Sam, and he didn't appear to be too happy about any of it. In fact, he looked really pissed off.

"Yeah! I'm 'poor Sam' now," Sam repeated.

Gus felt his smile quickly fade away. "I'm sorry, Sam. I should have never left you alone with them."

"Excuse me?" Emmy said. "What am I, chopped liver? He wasn't exactly alone with them. I was there."

"Oh jeez, what am I saying? Of course, Emmy. I'm so sorry. I shouldn't have left either of you alone with them. It was rude and selfish of me, and I apologize."

"Hey," Emmy said. "I'm used to it. I can handle myself, but 'poor Sam,'" she repeated, using air quotes, "has only just met them."

Gus turned to Sam again, and he couldn't quite read his expression this time, but he looked very uncomfortable at the least. "Sam, I'm really sorry."

"So I've heard," Sam retorted but added nothing more.

Gus tried to remember when Sam's mood had changed. They were fine in the dorm room getting ready. They were laughing and teasing when they'd left, made their way down the stairs, and crossed the quadrangle. Things seemed to change the minute they walked through the sally port. Suddenly it hit him. *Rav? Could she be right about Sam being jealous? I've got to find a way to tell him we're just friends.*

Emmy broke his concentration. "We've got to get back to the table before Dad comes looking for us, or we'll have hell to pay."

"Can you guys give Sam and me one minute?"

"No!" Emmy said. "You're not sending Beth Anne and me back to that table alone."

"Emmy's right," Sam finally piped up. "The sooner we get dinner out of the way, the sooner 'poor Sam' can get this night behind him."

Gus flinched, and he was sure his distress showed all over his face, but he couldn't help it. Sam's words cut him like a knife. *So much for Rav's take on Sam. Apparently he's not that into me.*

Then hurt gave way to anger. *Fuck it! It's not the first time he's gone off on you! Get over it, Gus, and let go of this stupid fantasy of you and Sam ever being more than friends. Hell, maybe not even that. Not as long as he's got that big fucking chip on his shoulder!*

Gus pushed his feelings down, schooled his expression, and said, "Sam's right. No need to drag this out any longer than we have to."

WHEN THEY returned to the table, Gus heard his mother and father already planning a big party in celebration of their "host cadet." They were absolutely giddy with glee. If his parents were normal, he would have taken pride in their offer to host Sam, but Gus knew it had nothing to do with being hospitable. They were doing it simply to impress all their friends and be acknowledged as the generous McRaes who always do the right thing. He would have been willing to overlook that if circumstances had been different, but Sam's reaction had ruined everything.

"I'd hold off on that party," Gus said as he sat down.

"Nonsense," his mother said. "I'm already picturing it in my head. We'll do a garden party in the backyard. The weather is breathtaking this time of year, isn't it, Angus?"

"Of course it is, dear," Gus's father replied. "And it sounds absolutely lovely. I'm already coming up with a guest list in my head. Of course we'll start with the Citadel alumni and go from there."

"No!" Gus said, a little louder than he'd planned.

His father gave him a very stern look, and his mother looked shocked and tearful.

"Here we go again," Gus heard Emmy whisper to Beth Anne. "Why does every family gathering have to end like this?"

Gus blocked Emmy and Rav out of his mind. "Sam doesn't want us to be his host family. And quite frankly, neither do I." Gus stood, wadded up his dinner napkin, and dropped it on the table in front of him. "This was an absolutely lovely evening. Thanks for ruining another special McRae meal."

"Angus!" his father said. "Sit back down."

"No!" Gus said, looking directly at his father, who appeared to be about to blow a major gasket. He then turned to Rav. "I'm sorry. I'm sure my parents will make sure you get home safely. Have a safe trip back to Spartanburg."

Beth Anne smiled weakly, and with that, Gus turned, tucked his cover under his arm, and walked right out of the restaurant.

MRS. MCRAE covered her mouth with her hand and started to cry. Mr. McRae patted her arm and then quickly pulled a white handkerchief from his inside coat pocket and offered it to her. Beth Anne and Emmy were looking everywhere but at Gus's parents, and the table was heavy with silence.

Seeing his only way out, Sam was the one to finally break that silence. "It was lovely to meet all of you, but I better go check on Gus." He stood. "This is not at all like him."

"I have no idea whether this is like him or not, son," Mr. McRae said. "I no longer know my own boy… or what's going on in that stubborn head of his."

"I'm sorry, sir. Ma'am," Sam said, dipping his head in Mrs. McRae's direction. "If you'll excuse me?"

"Wait!" Beth Anne said, taking Sam's hand and looking at Mr. and Mrs. McRae. "Would you mind terribly if I joined Sam? I may know a little about what's bothering Gus."

"By all means," Mr. McRae said. "Someone needs to talk some sense into that boy."

Beth Anne released Sam's hand, and he pulled out her chair as she stood. Happy to be away from Gus's parents, he put his hand in the small of Beth Anne's back and guided her in the direction of the front door.

As they dodged servers carrying trays of food, patrons coming and going, and the crowd of people near the front door waiting for a table, Sam wondered how in the hell this evening had turned into such a disaster. He felt badly for Gus having to deal with these people on a regular basis, but he was still pretty pissed at him. His plan, when he stood up from the table, was to look for Gus outside, and if he found him, head in the opposite direction.

Yes, he knew he would have to see him eventually, but for now he just wanted to be alone. *Actually, Sam, this is all for the best. You came to the Citadel to play football and get an education, not to suck up to the rich folks. You sure don't need the complications of a boyfriend. Especially a boyfriend with a girlfriend.*

Sam and Beth Anne finally made it to the foyer, through the double glass doors, and outside.

Sam stopped and waited. When Beth Anne didn't speak, he did. "So what's this all about?"

Beth Anne looked down and then back up, and their eyes met. "I may be way out of line here, but I don't think I am," she said hesitantly. She waited a few moments and then said, "He really likes you, Sam, and if I'm not mistaken, I think you like him as well."

Sam's heart dropped to the pit of his stomach and his chest tightened with panic. But he did his best to hold it together. *She can't mean...?*

"We're roommates," Sam blurted. "Of course we like each other."

"That's not what I mean, and you know it," Beth Anne said. "I'm gonna tell you something, and if I *am* wrong and you use my words against Gus, I will hunt you down and castrate you."

Sam instinctively covered his crotch with his hand but didn't say a word.

"Sam," Beth Anne said, looking around nervously as if to make sure no one was in earshot. "Gus is pretty sure he's gay. And... I've seen the way you look at him, and I believe you are too, or at least curious."

Sam staggered back as if he'd just taken a fist to the jaw. He heard the words Beth Anne was saying, but they were taking their own sweet time to sink in. *Gus's girlfriend is telling you he's gay and outing you at the same time!*

He saw a bench a few feet away, made his way to it, and sat with a thud. He covered his face with his hands and froze.

Beth Anne followed him and dropped down on the bench next to him. "Well? Am I right?"

Sam rubbed his face and eyes and then lowered his hands. He looked at Beth Anne. "But... I thought. You and he? You were...?"

"We're best friends. No more. I'm a lesbian, Sam."

"Wait? What do you mean 'Gus is pretty sure he's gay'?"

"Well," Beth Anne said, "he's never actually been with a guy, but he's been attracted to a few. And... he's really attracted to you. So."

"So what?" Sam asked, knowing what she was getting at.

"Are you gay, Sam?"

Sam hesitated. *Fuck! What do I have to lose?* "Yes. I'm gay," he whispered.

"Really gay?" Beth Anne asked. "Or just curious?"

Before Sam could answer, Beth Anne spoke again. "Because I don't want you cutting your teeth on Gus. If you hurt him, well, I've already told you what I'll do to you."

Sam covered his crotch again. "Really gay," he answered. "I've dated a couple guys."

"One last question," Beth Anne said. "Are you attracted to Gus?"

"Hell yeah," Sam said without hesitation. "But we're at the Citadel. Having sex with anyone is immediate grounds for expulsion. Let alone gay sex."

"Like I told Gus," Beth Anne said. "You won't be on campus all the time. That's why Gus was so happy when Emmy said the McRaes wanted to adopt you as a host cadet. That way you'd get to spend some time together off campus."

Duh! I never thought of that. "And I screwed that up royally," Sam mumbled.

"That you did."

"But there's no way to make this work. We're Knobs at the Citadel, for God's sake."

"Again," Beth Anne said, "like I told Gus, you can be model cadets on campus. But you can also be boyfriends off campus. If you want it to work, you can make it work."

"But we don't really know each other that well."

"Then get to know each other and see if there's something there. God! Why are guys such lugs?"

Suddenly Sam was filled with hope. "Okay! I've got to find Gus."

"Go," Beth Anne said. "But don't forget what I told you. You hurt him and you deal with me."

Sam leaned over and kissed Beth Anne on the cheek. "Thanks. And oh, does his family know?"

"Oh God no," she said. "They wouldn't understand. No one knows but me, so all of this stays between the three of us."

"Perfect," Sam said. "Gotta go."

CHAPTER TWELVE
MODEL CADETS

SAM RAN around the building and quickly scanned the long narrow parking lot. He spotted Gus standing at Concord Street with his hand held up in the air. Sam took off running in that direction, but before he could get to Gus, a pedicab pulled up. Gus and the driver exchanged a few words, and then Gus climbed in. Sam ran double time and just as the pedicab pulled away from the curb, he hopped in.

The driver stopped and looked back.

"Room for one more?" Sam asked.

"Jesus! Way to make an entrance," Gus said rather curtly, looking straight ahead. "And just what I need to really make this night a complete disaster."

The driver turned around and glanced at Gus, and Gus nodded. Then the driver focused on Sam.

Sam smiled and pointed to his riding companion. "I'm going wherever he's going."

The driver shook his head, looking dumfounded, but he started peddling and pulled out onto Concord Street, heading south.

"So where *are* we going?" Sam asked.

"Back to campus," Gus said, still without looking at Sam.

"Are you sure?" Sam asked.

"Oh yeah! I'm sure. I've had enough of all you people for one night, and I'm going back to the only place that's safe. Where I know what to expect."

"And speaking of making an entrance," Sam said, "that was quite the exit."

"Yeah, well! You met my parents. You blame me?"

"Not at all, but you could have made a bigger impact."

"How?"

"Oh, I don't know. Like maybe saying 'fuck you both' before you stormed out."

Gus almost smiled, probably imagining the looks on his mother and father's faces when he said the magic words, and Sam knew he was starting to have an effect on him.

"You wanna talk about it?"

"Nope," Gus said.

"Come on! Talking about them will probably make you feel better."

"What do you mean 'talking about them'?" Gus asked. "For the record, I've known who my parents are all my life, and I can deal with them. I'm more pissed off at you than I am at anyone."

"Me?" Sam asked.

Gus turned to look at Sam for the first time since he'd hopped into the pedicab. "Oh for fuck's sake. Don't act so innocent. You can be a real asshole sometimes. Correction. Most of the time."

"Ouch!" Sam said dramatically, pretending he was pulling a fake knife out of his chest.

Gus shook his head. "Such drama from a manly Citadel cadet."

"Well, aren't you the king of the one liners."

"Seriously, Sam, I just wish you would shut up so we can get back to the campus, forget this night ever happened, and get right back to hating each other."

"That's not very nice," Sam said. "And besides, I thought we liked each other now."

"Yeah, well, that was short-lived."

GUS WAS so pissed at Sam, he didn't say another word. But even in his anger and silence, he was very aware of Sam's knee, thigh, and shoulder brushing against his in the small seating area of the pedicab. Especially when the driver turned a corner or hit a bump. He caught himself thinking Sam was maybe even exaggerating the movements a bit.

Fuck, Gus! Stop this! It's over and done with. Let. It. Go.

As pissed as he was with Sam, he was even more pissed at himself. Mostly for allowing Rav to put such stupid thoughts into his head about the two of them. Like he and Sam could ever have anything more than a friendship, if that. He knew now that whatever weird exchanges they'd shared were nothing more than coincidences, and anything beyond that was all in his imagination.

The more Gus stewed in silence, the angrier he got. He'd thought enough of Sam to introduce him to his weird and controlling family and his best friend, and all Sam wanted to do was get the evening over with so he could be done with them. That really made his blood boil. *"Poor Sam,"* he heard Emmy saying in his head.

Poor Sam, my ass. The poor cadet from Detroit was offered a host family to take him in, feed him, and give him a refuge from the campus, and he turned it all down. So what if they were awful, controlling, social-climbing people who did it for all the wrong reasons. They at least made the offer, and he'd tossed it away like it was nothing.

For a split second, a tiny voice in the back of Gus's mind whispered that maybe he wasn't being entirely fair, but he was too pissed off for the thought to take hold.

The pedicab jerked and came to a stop. Gus looked up, and they were at the Hagood Gate. Gus got out of the cab, dug into his wallet, and gave the guy two twenties. He turned to walk away and Sam stuck a twenty into his hand.

"I pay my own way."

Gus took the twenty, shoved it into his pocket, stuck his chin against his chest, and started walking briskly. Knobs weren't allowed on any grassy areas unless they were in PT uniforms or in some sort of formation, so instead of cutting across Summerall Field, which would have been the shorter route, Gus turned left, entered the Knob lane, and followed the road around Summerall Field to the barracks. He could sense Sam behind him the entire way, but Gus never once looked back. He just wanted to get back to his barracks and for this day to be over with.

As his heart rate increased twofold with every step, Gus wasn't sure if it was the brisk walk or his anger at Sam forcing the blood to travel through his veins in double time. It suddenly occurred to Gus that he'd wasted way too many hours fretting over someone who obviously cared little for him or his feelings. That admission hurt more than anything, but at the same time, it brought a little closure to the stupid situation.

Gus tried blocking it all out of his mind, but by the time he got back to their room, he had worked himself into a complete frenzy. As he climbed the stairs, he imagined removing his cover and having steam shooting out of the top of his head. Every bad, mean, or hurtful thing Sam had ever said to him rushed through his brain like the swift currents of the Ashley River. *Fuck him! I'm done!*

The barracks seemed deserted. It appeared that most or all of the cadets were still out with their families or friends, celebrating the first night off campus, and Gus was fine with that. He pushed the door to their room open and tossed his cover onto his desk. The door didn't close behind him, and when he turned Sam was standing in the doorway, looking like a wounded bird. Gus bent down, untied his shoelaces, and toed off his shoes. He removed the rest of his uniform, hung it up, and put everything in his closet. After he finished undressing, Sam was still standing in the doorway.

"Are you gonna come in and close the door behind you?" Gus asked sarcastically. "Or are all the cadets going to get to see me in my underwear?"

SAM WAS sort of standing there more for effect than anything, but his eyes were glued to Gus's body. His stomach was ripped, and the muscles in his thighs were visible through the legs of his boxer briefs.

"Okay," Sam said. "If I close the door, will you at least talk to me?"

Gus shook his head. "I really don't think you want to hear what I have to say right now."

"I think you're wrong about that," Sam said, stepping in and allowing the door to close behind him.

Sam removed his cover and tossed it onto his bunk. He was tired of this cat-and-mouse game. Instead of untying his shoes, he brought his left foot up and tugged at his shoe until it came off. He tossed the shoe into the bottom of his locker, making quite the thud, and removed the right one much the same way.

He turned and rested his hands on his hips. "Are you gonna talk to me now?"

Gus didn't respond. He went to his closet, removed his toiletries bag, and headed for the door. Sam took two steps forward, put both hands on Gus's shoulders, spun him around, and backed him up against the door.

Their faces were so close Sam could feel Gus's warm breath against his face.

Sam slammed one hand against the back of the door while leaving the other one on Gus's shoulder. "Fuck, Gus! Yell at me. Curse me out. Do something. Don't just give me the silent treatment. You're not leaving this room until you talk to me."

Gus smiled incredulously. "So, what? You're gonna hold me hostage now?"

"If that's what it takes," Sam said.

"Fine! You want me to talk? Here goes. You are the most selfish bastard I've ever met. You've treated me like shit since the first day we met, and I'm not going to be your punching bag anymore. Please go to the Academic Officer and ask for a transfer. Tell him we're incompatible. I'll back you up on that one."

"I don't want a transfer," Sam said, his lips now inches away from Gus's.

"Why not?" Gus said quietly through clenched teeth, just in case there were any stray cadets roaming around in the hall. "You've done everything possible to offend me and my family. Why not move on to another cadet? Go ahead, man, share the charms of Stewart Adam Morley with the entire Citadel, one cadet at a time."

Gus glared at him, the normal bright silver-gray of his eyes now a dark, gloomy gray. "Furthermore, you can fuck with me all you want, but leave my crazy family out—"

Sam had heard enough. Before Gus could finish his sentence, Sam covered Gus's lips in a crushing kiss.

GUS WAS in the middle of a rant, really letting Sam have it, when suddenly he was mumbling into Sam's mouth. *Jesus! What the fuck? Is Sam kissing me? Really?*

Gus felt Sam's warm mouth pressed against his, and before he was able to adjust to that sensation, Sam's tongue was pressing against his lips for entry. Gus instinctively opened, and a warm exploring tongue slipped into his mouth. He felt the sensation all the way down to his toes. His toiletries bag hit the floor with a thud as he brought one hand up to rub over Sam's bald head and the other to wrap around the back of Sam's neck to pull him in closer. He needed more. Abruptly the anger disappeared, and Gus needed Sam nearer. He wanted their bodies tightly pressed up against each other, and he got what he needed. Gus had heard of people saying they'd seen fireworks on their first kiss, but he hadn't truly understood what that meant until now.

Sam had him pressed so tight against the back of the door, he couldn't move a millimeter, but he didn't care. It truly was the Fourth of July as explosions went off in his mind. He could even feel the vibrations as the fireworks erupted, sending streamers of color to the ground. Again and again he heard loud bangs, and then just as quickly as he had started, Sam stopped kissing him. *No! Don't stop. Please, don't stop, Sam!*

"Knobs! Surprise inspection! Now!"

Suddenly the banging made sense. It wasn't fireworks going off in his head; it was the Cadre banging on the other side of their door. His heart stopped beating, and panic filled every fiber of his being. He opened his eyes and saw the same dread and panic on Sam's face.

Somehow pulling himself together, Gus yelled, "Sir, yes, sir." *Okay. We can do this.* He took a quick look around. "Your cover. Put it on your head."

Sam ran back to his bunk, retrieved his cover, and slapped it on his head. They were both in sock feet. Sam was still in his uniform, but unfortunately Gus was in his underwear.

Gus bent down, picked up his toiletries bag, and put it in front of him. His erection was going down quickly, but not quickly enough. He wiped his lips, hoping they weren't too swollen from the heated kiss, and Sam followed suit. They both took deep breaths simultaneously.

"Ready, sir," Gus said, opening the door.

Two upperclassmen entered their room and eyed them both suspiciously. "Why are you back from leave so soon, Knobs?"

"No excuse, sir," Sam said quickly, taking a lesson from Gus.

"Why didn't your door open when I pushed against it?"

"I was on my way to the latrine when Cadet Morley came in. I was leaning against the back of the door as he told me about his leave. Sorry, sir!"

The Cadre eyed Gus suspiciously again and then moved on. One of the upperclassmen opened Sam's closet door. He pushed the clothes to one side, visually inspecting the closet, and quickly took note of Sam's dress shoes in the back where he'd tossed them earlier.

"Is this the way we keep our closet, Knob?"

"No, sir," Sam said.

"Why the mess, Knob?"

"No excuse, sir."

The Cadre pulled all of Sam's clothes and shoes out of the closet and tossed them to the floor. One of the upperclassmen opened Gus's closet door and peered in. He moved clothes from one side to the other, but luckily everything was as it should be. He slammed the door shut.

The other upperclassman went over to both bunks. They were taut and untouched except for where Sam's cover had landed, but fortunately it had only made a slight indention that was not really noticeable.

"Now clean up this pigsty before we have you out doing laps."

"Yes, sir," Gus and Sam said in unison.

The Cadre were gone as quickly as they had appeared.

GUS WALKED over to the door and once again rested his back against it. This time, a little weak in the knees, he slid down until his calves met the backs of his thighs and forced him to stop.

He sighed. "Man! That was close. What in the hell were we thinking?"

Sam stepped over his clothes, joined Gus at the door, stooped down, and placed his hands on Gus's knees. "I know what I was thinking. That was fucking hot. Gus, please tell me you felt something?"

"God, Sam! It was incredible. But something like this could get us expelled. We've got to be more careful."

Sam looked Gus right in the eyes. "I think that was the biggest adrenaline rush I've ever had. But you're right. We have to be more careful."

"That sort of came out of the blue. After playing games for so long, what finally brought it on?"

"Beth Anne."

"Rav?" Gus asked. "What does she have to do with this?"

"After you left the restaurant, she told me you thought you were gay and you really liked me. She also said she thought I was gay—or at least curious."

"And?"

"She was right on the money," Sam said. "I *am* gay."

Gus smiled. "Thank God for that. I thought I was going to be forever frustrated. But that meddling little lesbian. Wait until I get my hands on her."

Sam laughed. "Hey! I, for one, am grateful she said something. If she hadn't, who knows how much longer this game would have gone on?"

"Not long," Gus said. "I'd made up my mind it was stopping tonight."

Sam looked surprised. "What? Giving up on me that easily?"

"Look. A person can only take so much rejection."

"So are you?" Sam asked.

"Am I what?"

"Gay?"

"After that kiss," Gus admitted nervously, "I don't think there's any more doubt in my mind. But, Sam, I…." Gus hesitated.

"What?" Sam asked.

"I've—I've never been with anyone."

"Oh, that," Sam said.

"What do you mean 'Oh, that'?"

"Beth Anne told me that as well."

Surprised, Gus shook his head. "Damn, that girl has a mouth on her."

"Hey! She threatened to castrate me if I fucked with you."

"Now that's my girl."

"Oh! So it's okay to castrate me, but not okay to share your business?"

"Something like that," Gus said.

Sam leaned in and placed a long, gentle kiss on Gus's lips. Gus closed his eyes and enjoyed the wonder of Stewart Adam Morley. This time it was soft and sweet, not rushed and frantic. He enjoyed both equally, but he had so much more to learn.

When the kiss ended, Gus said, "Teach me more."

"In time," Sam said. "But not here."

"Where, then?"

"I think it's time I rethink that host family thing," Sam said. "That will give us a safe place to go off campus. But, Gus?"

"Yeah?"

"As much as I want you, I don't want to rush this. Okay?"

Gus nodded.

"I really want you to be sure before we take this to the next level."

"I'm already sure, but yes, we'll take it slow."

Sam stood, offered his hands to Gus, and pulled him to his feet. He looked around their room. "That's the last time I throw my shoes to the back of my closet in a fit of temper. I've got to clean up this mess."

"Correction," Gus chuckled. "*We* have to clean up this mess. I'm partly to blame, you know."

"I hardly see how, but I won't argue. Thanks."

AFTER THEY'D hung the last hanger, Sam's stomach let out a loud rumble. "Hey, we never did get to eat the dinner we ordered at Fleet Landing. I'm starved."

"I am too. Let's go get something! But...." Gus paused. "Oh, never mind."

"What," Sam asked.

"I was just thinking that if we go to the mess hall, we can't sit together," Gus explained.

"Then why don't we load up on snacks from the canteen and just come back here and hang out?"

"That sounds good to me."

"You gonna get dressed or go like that?" Sam asked.

Gus looked down and realized he was still in his underwear and black dress socks. "Oh. Nice look, huh? I forgot."

"I'm not complaining," Sam said. "The view is great from here."
"Give me a second to get dressed."

"No!" Sam said. "Just to keep you from putting on any clothes, I'll go and get a bunch of shit and bring it back."

Gus felt a blush creep up his neck to his face. "Are you sure?"

"Look at you blushing," Sam said, already putting his shoes back on. "Yeah. I'm sure."

Seconds later, he slipped out the door.

Gus sat at his desk, stunned over everything that had happened. *What a turn of events. Shit! Now I'm gonna have to apologize to my parents to make sure they adopt Sam as a host cadet. Oh jeez, and now we're gonna have to suffer through that party my mother is hell-bent on throwing. But it will all be worth it if I get to spend time with Sam off campus.*

Suddenly an unexpected wave of sadness came over Gus. He remembered they wouldn't get any overnights away from the campus until Thanksgiving break, which was still over two months away. Well, at least that would give them a little time to get to really know each other.

SAM DUMPED a large paper bag on his bunk and sat next to the pile of food. "Sorry, I didn't know what you liked, so I got plenty of everything."

Gus scanned the loot. Potato chips, corn chips, pretzels, cheese crackers, Snickers candy bars, Reese's peanut butter cups, and various sodas and juices. "Looks like you got it all covered."

Sam kicked off his shoes again and put them neatly in the closet. He sat on the edge of the bed and rummaged through their stash.

"Oh, hell no," Gus said.

"What?" Sam asked, giving him a questioning look.

"If I've got to sit here and eat in my underwear, so do you. So off with the clothes, cadet."

Sam smiled warmly, already unbuttoning his shirt. "You don't have to ask me twice."

Soon Sam was sitting cross-legged in the middle of his bunk with Gus sitting in the chair next to the bed, his feet propped up. They both figured this would be safer if the Cadre barged in again unannounced.

Gus popped the top on a soda. "We're gonna have to be a little more careful going forward."

"Tell me about it," Sam agreed, swallowing a mouthful of corn chips. "That was pretty close. But... I don't see anything wrong with this." He leaned over and gave Gus a peck on his cheek. "Or this," he said, turning Gus's face and kissing him gently on the lips. "Or this," he whispered, gripping the back of Gus's neck and pulling him close for a quick but crushing kiss.

When Sam retreated, Gus was breathless and dizzy. "They might find something wrong with that, but who the fuck cares?"

Sam smiled. "They'll have to catch us first, and that's never gonna happen." He stretched out on his bunk, pressed his socked foot against Gus's, and rubbed it back and forth.

Gus jumped at first and then relaxed into the new sensation.

"Ticklish," Sam said almost to himself. "I'm gonna make a point to learn something new about you every day."

Gus was warmed to his core. *He wants to know more about me.*

They ate in silence for the next few minutes, smiling back and forth occasionally until Gus broke the silence. "Sam?"

"Yeah?"

"Why now?"

"Why now what? The kiss?"

"The kiss, yeah. That's part of it," Gus said. "But this has been going on way longer than the kiss."

Sam nodded and took a sip of his soda.

"Oh hell. I don't know. We've been playing this little game, and I was starting to get very frustrated with it. I just couldn't decide if you were gay or not. I mean... I thought you were, but if I had made a move and you weren't, you might have been able to have me expelled. And I worked too hard to get here."

Gus leaned forward. "That doesn't really—"

Sam held up his finger. "Wait. I'm getting to your question."

Gus relaxed in his chair again and waited.

"I mean... I don't know if you remember this or not, but we saw each other on your matriculation day."

"I remember" was all Gus said.

"When our eyes locked, I was instantly attracted to you. Then we saw each other again at the beach house."

"I remember that too," Gus said.

"But my bus was pulling out, so I left without getting a chance to talk to you. And then when I opened the door and saw you were my new roommate, I knew I was fucked."

"Thanks a lot," Gus said, looking away.

"No!" Sam said. "Not like that. It was one thing to see you around campus and make pretty eyes at you, but to see you every day and live in the same dorm room—that was going to be tough. Have you *looked* in the mirror?"

Gus felt the blush creeping up his neck again. "I must see something totally different than you see, but thanks. So you still haven't really answered my question."

Sam smiled. "I'm getting to it, but you keep interrupting."

"Oh, sorry. Go on."

"Thank you. So just about when I'd decided you were as gay as a goose, I found out about Beth Anne."

"What does Rav have to do with any of this?"

"I didn't know she was Beth Anne at the time. All I knew was that Rav was someone special in your life. But at that point, I was fairly certain you were gay, so I figured Rav might be your boyfriend."

"Oh Jesus," Gus said.

"And when you introduced me to her, I put two and two together and figured she was Rav, short for Ravenel. Then after the two of you disappeared for, like, forever, I figured she was really your girlfriend. And then your parents started with the 'poor Sam' crap, and I got pissed at the entire situation."

"I'm sorry," Gus said, hanging his head.

Sam put his finger under Gus's chin and lifted his face until their eyes met. "So to finally answer your question, once Beth Anne told me you were gay, I guess I felt like I had nothing to lose. And you looked so damn cute leaning against the back of the door ranting and raving and going on and on about how badly I'd treated you and then standing up for your fucked-up family. I just couldn't help myself. I decided I'd use a creative way to shut you up. So there! That's why now."

"Nothing like taking the long way home," Gus said. "But I guess it worked."

"It did indeed."

This time Gus leaned up, looked at the door, and quickly pressed his lips against Sam's. "Thank you for explaining."

"I'll tell you anything you want to know if I get rewarded with a kiss at the end of each story. Hell. I'll even make stuff up."

Gus laughed and opened the pack of Reese's cups. He offered one to Sam. "Deal," he said. Then he sobered and dropped his head.

"What's wrong, Gus?"

"I'm just worried," Gus said. "I'm really attracted to you, and I hope you're attracted to me. But if you are, how do you see us navigating this minefield called the Citadel? Being gay here is not accepted behavior."

"Then we're not gay at the Citadel," Sam said. He pointed to the closed door. "I mean… behind that door we have a little freedom to steal a kiss or even a little more in the wee hours of the night, but outside of these four walls, we're model cadets. That's the bottom line. The Citadel encourages fellowship with other cadets, and outside of my football buddies, you're the cadet I want to spend time with."

"You make it all seem so simple," Gus said.

"It *is* that simple," Sam said, taking Gus's hand. "We're the only ones who can screw this up."

"I hope you're right."

"One day at a time," Sam said. "We can make this work. Together."

Gus liked the feel of Sam's hand in his. He felt stronger somehow and believed every word Sam was telling him. "You're right. We *will* make this work."

After a few more minutes savoring Sam's touch, Gus looked at the clock and started. "Jesus," he said. "It's almost ten thirty. We better get some sleep."

Sam smiled, and his eyes turned emerald green.

Gus stood, pulled Sam off the bed, and led him to the door. This time he positioned Sam with his back to the door and pressed his body against Sam's. At this point they were both in their underwear and Sam's growing erection pressed against Gus's. The feeling was remarkable and frightening at the same time. He smiled at Sam and quickly covered Sam's lips with his own.

Sam opened to him, and Gus felt like they were again one. Sam ran one hand over Gus's shaved head, as he had done before, and with the other, he gripped the back of Gus's neck. Then in one fluid move, he slid both hands slowly down Gus's back, slipped them inside the waistband of his briefs, and cupped Gus's ass. The sensation was odd and erotic at the same time, and Gus liked the hell out of it. But the dominance Sam had exhibited during their first kiss was now gone. Sam's touch was gentler, more tentative. He seemed fine allowing Gus to take the lead, and Gus was happy as hell about that.

When the kiss ended, they were both out of breath.

"Good night, Sam," Gus said, brushing Sam's cheek with the backs of his fingers.

"Night, Gus," Sam replied with a wink.

Gus leaned in and stole another quick kiss before he took a step back. They were both sporting erections, and before Sam moved, he wrapped his fingers around Gus's cock and gave it a brief squeeze. No one other than Gus had touched his cock since he'd been potty trained, and the touch of an unfamiliar hand, Sam's hand, sent chills up and down his spine.

Sam smiled and walked over to his bed. He put all the leftover snacks in the bag and stuck it in the back of his closet, then pulled the sheet and blanket back and climbed into his bunk.

Gus leaned over and kissed Sam one more time before climbing up into his own bunk and settling on his stomach. He hung one hand over the side, and just as he'd hoped, Sam reached up, took it, and squeezed.

"Sleep tight."

"You too."

Gus tried to settle down and get some shut-eye, but after tossing and turning for over half an hour, he realized sleep was not in his immediate future. He finally turned over onto his back and placed his hand over his heart. It was still racing, and come to think of it, his body was tingly all over. In the darkness of their small dorm room, he could feel the smile plastered all over his face. He must look, he decided, like a silly teenaged girl, but at the moment he didn't care. He soaked up the feelings and decided he never wanted them to end. *Euphoric. Yeah. That's a good word to describe it.* He likened his emotional state to the first time he'd masturbated so many years ago. The sensation had been overwhelming to a ten-year-old boy, yet that was exactly the way he felt right then. Except he wasn't ten years old anymore. He was a grown man. A man at a military college with a major crush on his roommate. But the intense combination of confusion and elation were as real now as they had been back then.

In an attempt to get his emotions in check, Gus closed his eyes and tried to breathe deeply and slowly. In and out. In and out. But after a few tries, the exercise proved to be in vain. His mind was drunk on a cocktail of exploration, fear, wonder, and yes… lust. He raised his hand and ran his finger over his lips. He'd just had his first real kiss, and it was so far beyond what he'd imagined it would be, he now thought he knew what crack addicts must feel like. If he wasn't careful, Sam could be *his* first real addiction, and that could prove to be very dangerous.

A section of the words of the Citadel Cadet Creed Gus had repeated at his swearing-in popped back into his mind. He mentally repeated them.

I will always endeavor to uphold the prestige, honor, and high esprit de corps of the Citadel and the South Carolina Corps of Cadets.

Never shall I fail my comrades. I will always keep myself mentally alert, physically tough, and morally straight….

"Morally straight," Gus whispered.

He and Sam had pledged their commitment to the establishment. He hadn't taken them lightly, and he didn't think Sam had either.

Suddenly Gus realized he and Sam, if he and Sam were to continue, would be headed for the biggest swim of their lives, stroke by stroke against the current.

No! I'm not going there. One day at a time, Gus.

Gus rolled over to his side. His fingers were still resting on his lips, and he again remembered the kiss. Sam was a great kisser. *He has so much more experience than me. I wonder how many guys he's been with or when he first realized he was gay.*

Gus smiled when he felt his mattress lift and what he imagined were Sam's bare feet pressed against his back and butt. "You wanna talk about it?" Sam asked in a playful voice.

Gus leaned over the side of his bunk. "What do you mean? Talk about what?"

"Jeez, Gus. You're tossing and turning up there like a major insomniac."

"Sorry," Gus said, offering Sam a weak smile. "It's just… my mind is racing, and I have so many questions."

"So? If you wanna ask, I'm an open book," Sam offered. "Ask away."

"Okay," Gus said. "For starters… when did you first know you were gay?"

"Well," Sam said, "I guess I felt different as far back as I can remember, but I had no idea why. I just knew it was true. I didn't even know what gay meant until I was a Cub Scout."

"Wait, you were a Cub Scout?"

"Yessss," Sam replied. "You got a problem with that?"

"No! Not at all. I was a Cub Scout too."

"No shit," Sam said. "My mom made me join. It was just after my stepdad left. She probably started realizing I was a little different and thought I needed a male influence in my life. Little did she know that's where my first homosexual experience happened."

"Seriously? In the Cub Scouts?" Gus asked. "Why couldn't I have been so lucky?"

Sam laughed. "Don't get too excited. It was on a camping trip, and it wasn't all that. It was just a hand job. Hell, we hadn't even reached puberty, but that didn't stop us. But the big problem came after the two guys I was with told the kids on the bus and at school that I jerked them off. Kids started picking fights with me, and I never knew why until much later that those guys had ratted me out but failed to rat themselves out. But you know…," Sam said, "I'm glad because it made me tough, and I learned how to defend myself early on."

A minute of silence followed before Sam went on. "Then there was the high school football team."

Gus's eyes widened. "You mean you blew a football team?"

"Not the entire team, you asshole," Sam replied. "But a few of the players. And they blew me. Hell. You have no idea what goes on in locker rooms when a bunch of horny adolescent teenaged boys get naked in the showers."

"Man, I so missed out on all of that," Gus said with disdain.

Sam chuckled. "And then there were the sleepovers."

"Sleepovers?"

"Yep. Word got out about the guys on the team who liked to suck dick, and that made me all the more popular. It's shocking how many jocks like to suck dick. I was amazed."

"How many guys have you been with? If you don't mind me asking."

"Oh, I don't know for sure. If you count the scouts and football team, maybe a half dozen or so, I guess."

"Wow!" Gus said. "I'm in awe."

Gus felt Sam's feet on his back again and let out a squeal when he flew off the mattress for a moment from the force. "Are you making fun of me?"

"Of course not."

"Are you sure?"

"I'm sure. I feel like I've missed out on so much."

"Not all of it was great," Sam said. "But your time will come… if I have anything to say about it."

"Will you teach me?" Gus asked, hanging his hand over the side of the bed again and feeling ecstatic when Sam took it and squeezed.

"Everything I know," Sam said.

Silence loomed between them for a few seconds. "I'm really scared, Sam."

"Of what? Sex?"

"No! Not the sex," Gus corrected. "Well, that's not totally true. Nervous about the sex, but terrified about how we're gonna be ourselves at the Citadel."

"Like I said. We're not going to be ourselves at the Citadel," Sam said. "We're gonna be smart and do what we have to do to make it to graduation. We'll have plenty of time to be ourselves later. We get our education now and take *us* one day at a time. I mean… when you think about it, nothing has really changed between us."

"What? Fuck yeah, things have changed," Gus said. "I've been crushing on you since the first time I saw you, and for some odd reason, fate has smiled upon me and now we're roommates. And it's also pure fate that you're as gay as I am. Jesus, I've never been this lucky in my life."

"Hey! Don't go counting your blessings too soon," Sam teased. "You don't know me that well."

"That's true," Gus said. "You can be a real asshole sometimes."

"There, see? You'll probably end up hating me, and all this will go away."

"Or we may end up liking each other very much, and life will get interesting."

"Or that too. Oh, and by the way, technically I'm not *as gay* as you are."

Gus frowned. "What?"

"I have a lot more experience, so I'm much gayer."

Gus howled. "Jesus. I've got so much to learn. Didn't know there were degrees of gayness."

"Yep," Sam said. "And again like I said, one day at a time. Now we better get some sleep, or we're gonna have a very bad day tomorrow."

Gus stuck his head over the bunk again and smiled. "Thanks for sharing."

"Anytime. Night, Gus."

"Night, Sam."

CHAPTER THIRTEEN
FIRSTS

"OH FUCK, noooo," Sam whined as the alarm clock started to blast.

"Make it stop," Gus begged from the top bunk.

Sam slapped the snooze button, rolled over, and buried his head under the pillow.

They both stole another seven minutes of shut-eye until the alarm sounded again. Sam slowly opened his eyes, resigned to the fact that they had to get up or Gus would be late for PT and he would be late for practice. He blinked a few times and focused on the indention in the springs above him.

Sam smiled. "Rise and shine, pretty boy," he said, positioning his feet where he thought Gus's ass would be and pushing upward.

"Noooo," Gus pleaded. "We just went to bed."

"We just went to bed because you felt like playing a million questions," Sam teased. "Was it all worth it?"

A few seconds later, Gus's face appeared over the side of the bunk, wearing a lopsided grin. "I believe it was."

"Well, then, now we pay the piper."

"You pay the piper," Gus said. "You have to be at practice thirty minutes before I have PT, so the way I see it, I've got a little more sleep in my future."

"Fine," Sam said, climbing out of bed and rummaging through his closet for his PT clothes. He was aware of Gus watching him very closely, his head resting on the edge of the mattress. When he glanced in Gus's direction and their eyes met, the look on Gus's face was one of pure admiration. And at that moment, Sam wanted nothing more than to climb into bed with Gus and spend the day teaching the cadet everything he wanted to know, education and football be damned.

But that fantasy lasted only a few seconds. The fact that this well-to-do, smart, funny, and very handsome cadet wanted him seemed beyond the realm of possibility, but Sam wasn't going to upset the apple cart. No way to know for certain where whatever they had stumbled upon was going from here, but he sure as hell was going to ride it all the way to the finish line if he could.

The only thing that bothered him was being someone's first. And he knew as sure as he was standing there that he would be Gus's first. It might not be today or tomorrow, or even in the next few weeks, but he was certain it would happen. With that came an unspoken responsibility, and that scared the shit out of him. *Come on, Sam. Everyone has to have a first.*

While Sam rummaged through his closet and dressed, he thought back to *his* first time. It had been with a friend of his best friend, Chris, who just happened to be gay as well. Chris had acted on it long before Sam ever had, but when Sam was finally ready to acknowledge who he really was, Chris had been right there to show him the ropes, so to speak. There had never been anything physical between the two of them, but one evening when they had gone out, Chris had taken it upon himself to hook Sam up with a friend. Sam remembered how scared he'd been. The guy was gorgeous and built like a brick shit house. Six feet five, about two hundred fifty pounds, and, as Sam later found out, hung like a horse to boot. But the guy had been very nice and especially patient with Sam. *I wonder what ole Dave is doing these days.*

Dave's had been the first dick Sam had put in his mouth, and he remembered being very surprised that it hadn't tasted like anything. He smiled at his naïveté, but he'd actually expected it to taste like dick or something. Whatever dick was supposed to taste like.

More importantly, it had also been the first time Sam had taken his first dick anally. Even though Dave had been very gentle, it had felt like he was trying to drive a Buick up Sam's ass. But in the end, Sam had had the most intense orgasm of his life and had shot his load clear over his head. His first sexual experience had been like a living, breathing wet dream, and even now Sam had goose bumps remembering how blissful he'd felt afterward. Like he was who he was supposed to be and finally living in his skin for the first time.

But what worried him the most about *his* first time was the emotional attachment he'd felt toward Dave. They'd dated for a couple of weeks, and Sam was certain he was in love with him, but when he told Dave how he felt, Dave fled, leaving him heartbroken. *Therein lies the problem, Sam.*

Sam had fallen in love with his first, or so he thought. He didn't think it was uncommon for that to happen, but it had been devastating for him at the time. Sam had been foolish enough to think they would be together forever, but the guy had other plans. It had been like taking a dagger to the heart.

And from what Sam knew about Gus, he was in the same vulnerable state that Sam had been in so many years ago. Sam knew Gus was willing and ready to take the plunge, but Sam also knew they had to proceed carefully.

"You wanna talk about it?" Gus asked, echoing Sam's words from the previous night.

Sam chuckled as he glanced at the door and then walked over to their bunk. He stole a quick kiss and touched the tip of Gus's nose with his forefinger. "Maybe later. Nothing important."

"Didn't look that way to me," Gus said. "Just promise me you'll let me know if I should be concerned."

"I promise."

WHEN GUS returned from PT, he showered and dressed for class. He had a few extra minutes, so he sucked it up and made the dreaded phone call to his parents to apologize for his behavior at dinner. While he waited for one of his parents to answer, Gus paced. For a split second, he almost wished he was still on cell phone restrictions, but that had ended after the first two weeks, and his parents were very aware of that. And besides, this was the only way to make sure his parents were still planning to adopt Sam as their host cadet, assuring Sam could join him for the Thanksgiving holiday. He hadn't actually asked Sam yet, but he was hedging his bets that when he did ask, Sam would say yes.

"Hello."

Gus cringed when his father answered the telephone instead of his mother, but he swallowed down the lump in his throat. "Morning, Dad."

"Angus," his father said.

"Can Mom pick up the extension? There's something I want to say to both of you."

"Hold on."

Gus heard his father's muffled voice as he apparently called out to his mother, then a click.

"Angus? Is everything all right?"

"Yes, ma'am." Gus swallowed hard. "I just wanted to apologize for my behavior at dinner. It was inexcusable. I was exhausted and stressed from Hell Week, and I took it out on my family and friends, and I'm sorry."

His mother sighed. "That's fine, dear. We understand."

Gus hesitated, knowing his father wasn't going to be so amenable.

"You're absolutely right. It was inexcusable," his father said in a harsh tone.

Here it comes, Gus. Brace yourself.

"But," his father continued, "I remember Hell Week like it was yesterday, and although you were completely out of line, it is somewhat understandable."

"Thank you for being supportive, sir."

"You get this one, Angus. But the next time you are disrespectful to your mother and me, there *will* be consequences."

"It won't happen again, sir."

"I'll count on that, Angus."

Before Gus could broach the subject of being Sam's host family, his mother interrupted. "Angus? How is that nice, underprivileged young man we met at dinner? What was his name again?"

"Sam?" Gus asked, crossing his fingers.

"No, that's not it. His name was Stewie or Stewman or something like that."

Gus rolled his eyes. "Oh, you mean Stewart. That's his given name, but he likes to be called Sam." Gus couldn't resist getting one small jab in. "Just like I prefer to be called Gus."

"Now, Angus," his mother said, completely ignoring the statement. "Your father and I want to become his host family, and we want to start at Thanksgiving."

"Yes!" Gus mouthed, giving his fist one pump in the air.

"Okay, Mom," Gus said calmly. "I'll ask him as soon as I see him."

"Now you be firm with him, Angus, and tell him your father and I will not take no for an answer," his mother said in a pouty voice. "This is important to our family, Angus."

And again Gus rolled his eyes. *Of course it's important to our family. If for no other reason than to show all of Charleston how generous you are to take in an underprivileged cadet.*

But not wanting to push his luck, Gus held his tongue.

"Oh, and one more thing, Angus," Gus's father said. "Your mother and Emerson are accompanying me to Spartanburg on the Sunday morning before Thanksgiving for a dinner later that evening honoring the law firm for some charity work we've been doing on behalf of battered women. I tried to pull a few strings to get you and your friend seats, but unfortunately the venue is quite limited, so you'll have to fend for yourself for one night. We'll be back on Monday afternoon."

Oh my God! This can't get any better. An entire night in the house alone with Sam.

"Oh! Don't worry about us. We'll manage just fine."

"I'm sure you will," Gus's father said.

Gus cleared his throat. "I've got to go now. I have class in five minutes, and I don't want to be late."

"Okay, honey," his mother said. "I love you."

"Love you too, Mom. Bye, Dad."

"Bye, son."

Gus ended the call. "Wow! That worked out way better than I expected."

SAM FINISHED football practice at the normal time and headed back to the dorm. Three days a week the cadets got two hours of downtime between class and dinner to study or do homework. Most Knobs, including him and Gus, studied in the library. But today as Sam climbed the stairs to their room, he was hoping Gus had maybe had the same idea as he had and returned to the dorm to study instead. As he entered the hall, he scanned for any signs of the Cadre or other cadets milling about, and much to his surprise, the dorm seemed almost deserted. That suited his needs just fine. It might afford him the few minutes he needed to scratch an itch he'd had since he'd woken up that morning.

He opened the door slowly and looked inside with much anticipation. *Yessss!*

Gus looked up from his desk, where he was sitting with an open book in front of him. When their eyes locked, a smile consumed Gus's face. Sam's heart skipped a series of beats, and it almost took his breath away. No matter how hard he'd fought, he realized right then and there that there was no way he was going to win this battle. Gus couldn't help but be hot, and Sam's proverbial goose was cooked.

Throwing caution to the wind, Sam stuck his head back out into the hallway and looked both ways. *The coast is still clear.* He closed the door behind him, dropped his backpack on the floor, and walked over to Gus. He took the cadet by the hand and led him to the door.

He pressed Gus against the back of the door and rested his forehead against Gus's. "I was hoping you'd be here."

"I came back here instead of the library, hoping you might do the same."

Sam smiled and nodded.

Sam had already accepted the fact that as long as they were at the Citadel, they would get nothing more than a few stolen moments here and there. But he'd also vowed to himself to take advantage of every opportunity he could get to be close to Gus.

He quickly covered Gus's mouth with his own, and when he sought entry for his tongue, Gus wantonly opened to him. Gus ran his hand over Sam's head, cupped the back of his neck, and pulled him closer. Sam's heart raced as he deepened the sloppy kiss, pleased that Gus was holding his own. Gus wanted him. That was evident. But the fact that they could get caught at any moment added another element to the excitement.

In a surprise move, Gus dropped his hands, placed one on each of Sam's asscheeks, and pulled hard, forcing their erections to crush together. Sam moaned into Gus's mouth, hopefully conveying his desire, but then gasped when Gus reached around with his left hand, grabbed a handful of Sam's crotch, and squeezed hard.

Sam's knees buckled, and he almost lost his balance, but Gus's strong right hand still had a grip on Sam's ass, holding him in place. With all the emotions and testosterone flowing between them, Sam almost shot his load in his pants like an adolescent.

Sam was totally lost in the moment. It was just him and Gus and be damned to the world. He was about to lift Gus off the ground and carry him to the bed when the loud noise of a door slamming made them both jump. The noise brought him back to reality and must have done the same for Gus. They broke the kiss and froze. Then Gus released his grip on Sam and raised his hands in the air. Sam did the same, his heart still racing. Gus bolted for his desk chair, and Sam dove and landed on his bed.

Closing his eyes, Sam linked his fingers over his chest and did the best he could to slow his heart rate. He opened one eye slightly and peeked at Gus, who was staring at his open book as if it held the answers to all the world's problems.

After a few more silent moments passed and the Cadre didn't burst through the door, Sam opened both eyes wide and looked in Gus's direction.

Sam released the breath he'd been holding, and Gus smiled and whispered, "Fuck! That was risky."

"But soooo worth it," Sam replied.

Gus smiled and gave Sam an agreeable nod.

"Either you've been holding out on me, or you're an extremely quick learner," Sam whispered.

Gus's face turned beet red. "I'm sorry. I don't know what came over me. I guess it was years of dreaming of a moment like that and then actually experiencing it. I just sort of let go, and my libido took over."

"Don't apologize," Sam quickly said. "That was fucking hot."

Gus's blush deepened to yet another level of red, but to his credit, he didn't look away.

Sam held his gaze. "I almost came in my pants."

Gus smiled and shook his head. "I was right there with you," he said as he picked up his book and scooted his chair over to their bunk, where Sam was still lying. Sam looked at the book.

"In case the Cadre barge in," Gus said. "It'll look like we're studying together."

"Good idea."

Sam hopped off his bed, grabbed his backpack, and jumped back into his bunk. He kicked off his shoes, and they hit the floor with a thud. He dug through his pack and retrieved a textbook, stretched out, and laid the open book across his stomach.

"There."

Gus stood, gathered Sam's shoes, and placed them neatly in the bottom of Sam's locker. "Better safe than sorry," he said, apparently remembering their last interaction with the Cadre.

"Oh, right," Sam said. "Thanks."

While he was up, Gus toed off his shoes as well, placed them in his locker, and again took his seat.

His book in his lap, he rested his socked feet on the steel bedframe and smiled warmly. "I think we're in pretty good shape now."

"We can do this," Sam said. "As long as we stay smart and don't get carried away."

"Like we did just then?" Gus asked.

"Sort of," Sam agreed. "But man, it really was worth it."

"Speaking of *worth it*," Gus said, "I talked to my parents this morning."

Sam raised an eyebrow. "And how did that go?"

"Well," Gus said, "for starters… and I'm pretty sure after that dinner fiasco this isn't going to be at the top of your to-do list, but they still want to be your host family."

Sam's initial thought was the same as it had been when Gus's parents suggested it at dinner: *Oh, hell no!*

But before he had a chance to say "Thanks, but no thanks," Gus spoke again. "But…," he said hesitantly, holding up his index finger, "before you say no, they invited you to stay with us for the entire Thanksgiving break."

Oh, double hell no! Sam didn't think he could get through a whole week with Gus's parents without killing at least one of them. He was about to decline when his brain kicked in and registered what Gus had said. *I'd get to spend an entire week with Gus outside of the prying eyes of the Citadel.*

"Okay," he blurted out before he could stop himself.

"Okay?" Gus repeated.

"Sure," Sam said. "It's worth putting up with your parents to get to spend a week with you away from here."

Gus's face lit up like a Christmas tree. "Then you're gonna like this even more."

Now Sam was really intrigued.

"Mom, Dad, and Emmy are going to Spartanburg on Sunday morning and won't be back until Monday afternoon."

"You mean we get an entire night alone?"

Gus nodded. "Just the two of us."

A smile crept across Sam's face. He laid his hand on top of Gus's foot and squeezed. "That's gonna be so great."

"I know," Gus agreed. "And Sam?"

"Yeah?"

"I hope you'll consider being my first."

Now Sam was torn. He'd had a pretty good idea this was coming, and he wanted it badly, but now it was a definite reality. On one hand he wanted to scream yes at the top of his lungs, but on the other hand, he was scared shitless. *If I'm his first and we really are compatible… that comes with strings. Strings that maybe neither of us can handle. For the next three plus years, our lives won't be our own. I can't imagine negotiating the Citadel and a secret relationship.*

Sam felt Gus's eyes on him, and when he looked up, Gus's head was tilted to one side, and he was studying Sam intently. Sam tensed up. *How in the hell am I gonna explain what I'm feeling?*

"Okay, Sam, spill it. You have the same expression on your face you had this morning."

Sam scrambled to come up with something to say to avoid the truth, but he went totally blank. He looked at the door and back at Gus. *Oh, fuck it!*

He scooted to the end of the bed and took Gus's hands in his. "Look. I'm just a little scared, okay?"

Gus looked at the door and then down at their joined hands. "Of what?"

Sam hesitated. *What am I afraid of exactly?*

"Oh hell, Gus. I don't know. Liking you too much. You liking me too much. Being your first. I'm scared shitless about all of this."

Sam let go of Gus's hands, stood, and started pacing. Out of habit, he reached up to play with his hair and then remembered he didn't have any. *Shit!*

"Gus, I like you," Sam said. "I like you a lot. And I want you as much as I like you, if not more, but our lives won't be our own until we graduate. What happens if *this*," he said, gesturing between the two of them, "works? Can we handle it? Can we make it work, not get caught, and make it to graduation?"

Gus stood and grabbed Sam by the shoulders to stop him from pacing. "Of course we can."

"What if we can't?" Sam whispered.

"I think we can," Gus reassured him. "But I think you're getting way ahead of yourself."

"What do you mean?"

"Hell, Sam," Gus said through a weak smile. "You might hate being with me, and in that case, *this*"—Gus mimicked Sam's hand gestures between them—"wouldn't be a problem."

"Why would you say that?" Sam asked.

"Come on. You are way more experienced at all of this than I am. You might decide I'm not worth the trouble."

Sam chuckled nervously. "Somehow I doubt that's gonna happen."

"And one more thing. About being my first," Gus said. "Don't give that a second thought. I mean... everyone has to have a first, right? And I really want mine to be you, but if you don't want the same thing, I understand. I'm a big boy. Really! I can handle it."

Sam took Gus by the hand, dragged him to the back of the door again, and kissed him deeply. When the kiss ended, he rested his forehead against Gus's. "I want to be your first, but...."

"But what?"

Sam hesitated. "I guess the only way to put it is that it's a very emotional experience. At least it was for me, and I'm a little afraid of the responsibility that goes with that."

Gus studied him closely. "What responsibility?"

Sam hesitated, trying to find the right words. "I want it to be perfect for you, and if your first is anything like mine, you're gonna have all sorts of feelings to deal with."

"It's just sex," Gus said.

"See! That's what I'm talking about," Sam said. "I thought the same thing, but it was so much more than just sex, and looking back now, I wasn't prepared for it. I mean… the act itself went fine, but the way I handled it afterward didn't go so well."

Gus sighed. "I still don't get what the big deal is."

"The big deal is for the first time you're giving another person access to your most intimate parts. Physically and emotionally."

Gus looked like he was starting to get it but wanted to know more. "Tell me about your experience."

Sam looked up at the ceiling and sighed. *Why is this so fucking hard?*

"It's okay if you don't want to talk about it," Gus said. "I understand."

"No!" Sam said. "I do. But I can't seem to find the right words."

"Just talk to me, Sam. It'll be okay."

Sam sighed. "Okay. After we, well… you know."

"You mean had sex? Made love?"

Sam rolled his eyes. "Yes…. Anyway, I felt so free and liberated. It was like all the emotions I'd buried for most of my life somehow finally made their way to the surface. And for the first time, I felt like I was being the person who I was meant to be. But instead of understanding what was happening to me, I transferred those emotions to the person I was with and mistook the feelings for love."

"So you fell in love with your first?"

"Yeah. Hard. And the guy didn't return the feelings. It didn't end well for me."

"I'm sorry."

Sam cupped Gus's face in his hands. "So you see? I like you a lot, I really do. But we're just starting out with whatever this is, and neither of us have any idea where it's heading. If we choose to take this further, none of it will be easy, considering where we are, and if either one of us can't handle the stress of it all and it doesn't work out, I just don't want you to experience the pain I went through." Sam paused. "God! I know this is all coming out wrong."

Gus pressed his lips against Sam's and kissed him softly.

"You don't want me to get hurt. I get that. But, Sam, I'm gonna eventually fall in love, and I'm gonna get hurt too. That's part of life, and there is no getting around it. But I told you, I'm a big boy. If one day *we* decide to pursue a relationship and fall in love, that will be incredible. But whether you're my first or not, if our feelings aren't mutual, I don't want any part of it."

Gus looked down at Sam. "How old were you when you lost your virginity anyway?"

"Seventeen."

"Sam, we're twenty years old now and a lot more mature than we were when we were seventeen. I think—no, I *know* we can handle it."

Sam sighed and rubbed the back of his neck. "Maybe you're right. I guess I'm just freaking out a little."

"Relax," Gus said. "I have an idea."

"What's that?"

Gus smiled. "What if I go out and find someone else to be my first? That way by the time you have me, I'll already be soiled, and you'll be totally off the hook."

"No fucking way!" Sam said before he had time to think about it.

Gus laughed. "I'm just teasing. Well, sort of," he said, replacing Sam's hand with his own and kneading Sam's shoulders. "Look. We've got a couple of months to decide if we want to take this to the next level or not. And besides… if we decide to just be friends, I've been a virgin for this long, another few years won't kill me."

Voices outside their door brought them back to their reality, and they made beelines for their previous positions. When they were settled, Sam again rested his hand on the top of Gus's foot.

"I'm sorry I freaked out a little."

"I get it," Gus said, wiggling his toes. "I'm nervous about it as well. What if I suck at being gay? No! Wait! Don't answer that. Bad choice of words."

Sam laughed out loud. "If you *don't* suck, *that* could be a problem."

"Good point."

Chapter Fourteen
Behind a Closed Door

For all Gus's talk about having plenty of time, the next couple of months seemed to go by in a flash. The days were filled with more PT, academic classes, parades, drills, study time, and for Sam, the extra element of football practice and football games.

Football was a big deal at the Citadel, and Sam was an exceptional player. Gus loved going to the games and watching Sam play, but what he most treasured were the moments he and Sam continued to steal whenever they could. And with each day, the desire between them seemed to grow stronger and stronger. Over the last two months, they'd spent more time against the back of their door than they had any other place on campus. It was their only semisafe spot, and they took advantage of it every chance they got. As the days passed, the surprise visits by the Cadre lessened, and things settled down dramatically, which gave them a little more freedom—or at least the illusion of it.

The Friday before Thanksgiving, Gus woke long before dawn and lay waiting for the alarm clock to go off. He listened to the sweet sounds of Sam's light whimpers coming from the bunk below, a sound he'd happily grown accustomed to over the last couple of months.

As of 1500 hours, it would officially be Thanksgiving break. Gus's heart raced and goose bumps covered his body when he thought about their long-awaited alone time together. They hadn't made a conscious decision to go through with it, but they both knew it was inevitable.

A full thirty-plus hours completely on their own. Gus closed his eyes and thought about what he wanted to do to Sam during those hours. Although he hadn't actually done any of it yet, he'd seen enough Internet porn to know exactly what went where, and he was more than ready to put it all to the test. His cock jumped from just thinking about Sam that way, and his morning erection grew in size and intensity. He wrapped his long fingers around his length and squeezed. Closing his eyes, he pictured Sam riding him, feeling the heat of Sam's tight ass surrounding him.

Two months ago he couldn't even have imagined thinking along these lines, but his comfort level with Sam had certainly grown over that time, and as nervous as he was, the nervousness was now mixed with anticipation and excitement.

"I hear you up there," a sleepy voice said from the bunk below. "Are you whipping your pud?" Sam asked.

"No!" Gus said without thinking.

"Are you sure?"

"Well, maybe just a little."

Sam chuckled. "At least please tell me you're thinking about me."

"On the flesh," Gus said.

"Don't you mean in the flesh?"

Gus was feeling a little daring with his hand wrapped around his cock, enjoying Sam's imaginary ride. "Nope. Right about now you're on the flesh. My flesh, that is. And you're riding it nicely."

"Oh, man, I like where this is headed," Sam whispered.

Within seconds Sam's head popped above the bunk. He looked at Gus's tented sheet with an expression of pure desire, and then he glanced at the door.

"Don't even think about it," Gus said in a soft voice. "We've come too far to get expelled the day Thanksgiving vacation starts."

Sam grabbed Gus by the hand and tugged. "Out of bed. Now."

Gus smiled, climbed out of his bunk, and headed for their spot. He put his ear to the door, but it was still early. He heard no activity in the hall.

Sam turned Gus around and plastered him against the back of the door, buried his head in Gus's neck, and ground his own erection against Gus's. "Damn, you feel good. I don't know if I can wait until Sunday."

"I guess that unease and burden of responsibility you had a couple of months ago have both faded away," Gus whispered sarcastically.

"At times like this," Sam whispered against Gus's neck, "I couldn't give a fuck about responsibility."

In a flash Sam licked his way down Gus's torso and wrapped his mouth around Gus's cotton-clad cock.

Gus hissed and threw his head back so hard, the thud echoed through their tiny room, as well as the hall outside their door. He slipped both his hands into Sam's armpits and pulled him back up to him.

"Fuck, Sam. You're gonna get us expelled."

"But what a way to go, huh?"

Sam covered Gus's lips in a crushing kiss. When the kiss ended, Sam's beautiful hazel eyes were staring into his. "That will have to hold you."

And with that Sam grabbed his dopp kit from his locker, pulled the door open, and slipped out of the room, leaving Gus breathless and horny as hell. *Fucker!*

Right after they'd started this little lust affair, they'd showered together a couple of times and were both badly bruised from pinching themselves over and over again to keep their erections at bay. So it was either stay black and blue or not shower together, and they had decided on not showering at the same time to avoid calling any attention to themselves.

Gus was still standing against the back of the door—experiencing severe afterglow and remembering the feel of Sam's warm, moist lips surrounding his length—when the alarm clock sounded, scaring the shit out of him. Annoyed, he walked over, slapped the top, and climbed into Sam's bed. He still had thirty minutes, and he wasn't quite ready to let go of what had just happened. He buried his face in Sam's pillow and inhaled Sam's unique scent, which made his cock jump with excitement again.

Gus reached behind him and removed the small bottle of lube he knew Sam kept in his bedside table. He stretched out on his back, tucked the waistband of his underwear under his balls, squeezed a little lube into his palm, and took himself in hand. He closed his eyes and pictured Sam riding him like a bronco. He imagined Sam's warm, wet heat moving up and down, surrounding his cock while their lips were pressed together tightly.

Gus held on as long as he could, but he was only a few strokes away from losing it all. He stopped for a second to regain some kind of control, but then he remembered the sight of the top of Sam's head when he'd taken Gus into his mouth earlier. That was all he needed to fall over the edge.

Gus made it through two more strokes, and then the battle was lost. The first shot sent his load up and almost over his left bicep. The second and third covered his abs, and he milked the last of his release until his fingers were covered. Now sated, Gus opened his eyes and gasped when he saw Sam standing alongside their bunk.

"That was beautiful," Sam said, running two fingers over Gus's chest and scooping up the remains of his seed. He brought his fingers to his lips and licked them clean. "And also delicious," he added.

Gus could feel heat once again creeping up his face, but he fought the urge to bolt. He even did his best to give Sam a seductive smile since Sam seemed to be enjoying the show.

Sam sucked on his fingers and then turned to his desk, pulled a few tissues out of the box, and handed them to Gus. "You better get cleaned up before you head to the showers. That place is a zoo."

"Thanks," Gus said, climbing out of Sam's bunk and tossing the soiled tissue in the trash can by the bed. He turned and headed to his locker, doing the walk of shame right past Sam without stopping. Gus jumped when Sam grabbed him by the arm and spun him around. He cupped the back of Gus's neck and brought their lips together in a sloppy, wet kiss.

When the kiss ended, Sam whispered, "That was the hottest thing I've ever seen." He slapped Gus on the ass. "Now hit the showers, cadet."

WHEN GUS returned, he was stunned to see Sam was still there. Sam must have recognized his surprised expression. "I just wanted to say good-bye and thank you again for the show."

Gus felt the blush again creeping up his face. "You're welcome," he managed to say with a straight face.

"I'm really looking forward to our time off, and especially our private time."

"Me too," Gus agreed. "But you know we still have to spend some time with my dysfunctional family as well as get through that stupid party my mom is throwing."

"Yeah. That part will suck," Sam said. "But so worth it to get to spend some alone time with you."

"I agree."

"Okay, I need to get to practice, but I'll see you back here right after lunch."

This time it was Gus who moved Sam to the all too familiar spot. Gus could hear cadets coming and going right outside their door, so he knew he'd have to make this one quick. He backed Sam up against the door, cupped his face, and planted a big one on him. Sam in turn wrapped a hand around the back of Gus's neck and pulled him closer.

"Now, now," Gus said with a wink. "Let's save some for next week. You're dismissed, cadet. Have a great practice."

Sam flashed a sinister smile, gave Gus a quick peck on the cheek, and was out the door in a flash.

Gus sighed, rested his hands against the back of the door, and dropped his head in frustration. He knew this was all they had right now, and it wasn't going to get much better. They had Thanksgiving week and hopefully Christmas vacation, but if they chose to pursue a relationship, it was going to be this way for the next three years. He stayed in that position for a few minutes, thinking about what was coming. This week would undoubtedly make or break them. Being with Sam? He'd never been so sure of anything in his life. But that didn't mean he wasn't nervous.

Spending time with Sam these last few months had been great, but he'd never felt especially nervous or scared because he knew it could only go so far. It had always stopped before it progressed past the point of no return. That was their reality. But this time it was going to be different. There would be no stopping until it was over. He trusted Sam, and he knew deep down Sam would be patient with him, but that still didn't alleviate the anxiety.

On one hand, he was as ready as he'd ever been to be with a man. To be with Sam. But on the other hand, he was scared to death. Sam had inched his way into Gus's heart as surely as he was standing there, and if he was not good or Sam was disappointed, it could very well be the end of them. *Be careful, Gus. Remember what Sam said about falling in love with his first. You can't let on that you're practically there! You have to be cautious.*

Gus hit the back of the door with his fist. *Stop this! None of this speculation is going to do anything except make you more nervous. Like you told Sam. You're a big boy, and you're gonna be fine, whatever happens. Just enjoy yourself and the experience.*

Gus froze when he heard whistles and the stomping feet of the Cadre. He looked down and noted he was still in his towel, so he quickly moved to his locker, taking in the room at the same time. Besides him not being dressed, everything looked like it was in place. He pulled on his PT clothes and his athletic shoes and slowly opened his door. The Cadre was torturing two cadets across the hall. Gus slipped out unnoticed and headed for the stairs.

PT WENT as expected, and the day's classes were uneventful because of the impending holiday. Even the Cadre seemed a little laid-back at lunch. No quizzes, no interrogation. Nothing.

By the time Gus got back to their dorm room, Sam was in uniform and lying on his bunk with his packed bag beside him.

"Hey!"

"Hey back," Sam said.

Gus smiled. "How did you make it back here before me?"

"The coach let us off early, so I came back, showered, and packed."

"Nice," Gus said. "Did you remember to pack your dress whites? My mom will die if she can't parade us around in uniform for her party."

Sam nodded and pointed at the back of the door, where his uniform was hanging along with Gus's.

"You got mine out too?" Gus asked.

"I hope you don't mind," Sam said. "I had nothing else to do, and I knew you'd need it, so I got it ready for you."

"Mind?" Gus said. "Of course not. Thank you."

"Do you have any civilian clothes to take?" Gus asked.

"No," Sam said. "I left all that in Michigan. But... I thought maybe your parents might want to buy me some new clothes since I'm so underprivileged and all."

"Ha," Gus said. "Knowing my mom, she may just do that."

"No!" Sam said. "I was only teasing. Do. Not. Let. Them. Do. That."

"I'll tell them. But don't worry, I have plenty. You can borrow some of mine."

"We're not exactly the same size," Sam said, looking up at Gus.

"True, but my workout shorts and T-shirts will do just fine."

Gus was aware of Sam watching his every move as he threw some things in a bag. "Is everything all right?"

"Everything's great," Sam said. "I'm just imagining what it's gonna be like having you naked without worrying about being caught."

Again Gus could feel heat creeping up his face, but he smiled nonetheless. "That part is going to be so cool."

"God, I love it when you blush," Sam said.

"Oh jeez! Is that why you make me do it so much?"

"Exactly," Sam said. "Hey, what time are your parents picking us up?"

"Actually Emmy is picking us up. She just got her driver's license, and she convinced my parents to let her come alone."

Sam sat up. "If she kills us before I get to have my way with you, I'm gonna be extremely pissed."

"Tell me about it," Gus agreed. "But luckily we don't have that far to go."

"Hey, Gus," Sam said while Gus was still throwing things in his bag, "what kind of plans does your mother have for us next week?"

"Let's see," Gus said, looking up at the ceiling. "Tonight is just the family. Tomorrow is our coming-out party, so to speak, and Sunday is church and then brunch. Then the only other scheduled thing I know about is Thanksgiving dinner. That will be a big to-do with about twenty people. Other than that, we are on our own."

"What will we do with our time?" Sam asked.

"Other than Sunday and Monday when we'll be naked all day and night," Gus said with a wink, "whatever we want. We can take the four-wheelers to the beach, take my dad's boat out and do a little fishing… or maybe we can even find a way to have another night alone!"

"That all sounds great except the 'another night alone part,'" Sam said. "Let's wait to see how Sunday and Monday goes before we plan that."

Gus's heart dropped to the bottom of his stomach. "Oh, okay," Gus said, turning away so Sam couldn't see the hurt on his face. "I guess I shouldn't have assumed anything."

Gus saw Sam's reflection in the mirror. He jumped out of his bunk and ran to Gus. "No! You goofball," he said. "I was just teasing you."

Gus closed his eyes and smiled as Sam drug him to the back of the door and kissed him gently. "I'm sorry. Sometimes my mouth works before my brain can catch up. Seriously, Gus, I would love another night alone with you. I'm sorry for being an ass."

"It's okay," Gus said. "I guess I'm still a little nervous."

Sam kissed him again. "Don't be. It's going to be fantastic. You'll see."

Gus closed his eyes and wrapped his arms around Sam's neck.

Without warning they were both propelled across the room when the door burst open. "Surprise inspection," two members of the Cadre said in unison.

Gus looked at Sam, and they were both speechless.

The Cadre eyed them suspiciously. "What in the fuck were you doing behind this door, cadets?"

Gus spoke, thinking quickly on his feet. "Getting our uniforms ready, sir," he said, pointing at the dress whites hanging behind the door. "My parents are Cadet Morley's host family, and they are throwing a party in our honor and asked us to wear our dress whites."

"Well, isn't that sweet," one of the Cadre said.

"A party in their honor," the other one said.

The Cadre glanced around the room, apparently looking for anything they could use to penalize them, but luckily everything was in place except Sam's packed duffel on his bunk and Gus's on the floor.

Obviously annoyed that everything was in place, the Cadre said, "Drop and give me twenty, cadets. Just for the hell of it."

Gus saw Sam open his mouth to protest, but he elbowed Sam and glared at him with an awful mien. Gus hoped his expression said everything he couldn't say. It must have because Sam dropped, as did Gus, and they did twenty push-ups simultaneously and then stood at attention waiting for their next order.

"Anything else, sir?" Gus said.

"Now get your shit and get the fuck out of here," one of the upperclassmen said. "Happy fucking Thanksgiving."

"And enjoy your party," the other said sarcastically.

Sam grabbed his duffel and uniform from the back of the door and handed Gus his. Gus scooped up his duffel, and they were out of there in a flash.

When they hit the stairs, Gus started laughing. He could see Sam was still pissed, but he didn't care. The farther they got, the harder he laughed. By the time they got to the street, Sam's scowl had turned into a smile, and then they were both laughing so hard they could hardly catch their breath.

"That was so close," Gus said, bent over nearly in half and holding his stomach.

"I know," Sam agreed. "We were almost busted."

"Thank God you hung those uniforms on the back of the door," Gus added.

"And that you were quick enough to come up with that lame story."

"Hey," Gus said, "that was nothing short of genius."

"Okay, it was genius. But we're still gonna have to be more careful."

"You're right," Gus said, finally calming down and starting to catch his breath. "But I do feel a little guilty lying to the Cadre. Honesty is part of the oath we took and the Cadet Creed."

Gus took a seat on the curb, and Sam sat next to him. Sam's voice took on a more serious tone. "Fuck that shit, Gus. We're not doing anything wrong. If they wouldn't be so fucking homophobic," he said. "I mean… it's not like we're stealing or hurting anyone. What the fuck do they have against falling in—" Sam stopped short of finishing his sentence and looked away.

Gus's mouth dropped open. *Was he going to say falling in love?*

"Sam?"

Sam cleared his throat. "Yeah?"

"Will you please finish your sentence?"

Sam was now looking down at the ground. Gus watched him pick up a little stick and start drawing circles in the road dust. But he still didn't answer Gus.

Gus decided to leave it alone. *Maybe I just heard wrong.*

He watched silently as Sam continued to draw various shapes in the dirt.

Moments later Gus sucked in a breath when Sam drew a heart and turned to look at him. Sam smiled weakly. "—against falling in love," he whispered. "What the fuck do they have against falling in love?"

"Are you saying what I think you're saying?" Gus asked.

Sam smiled and rolled his eyes. "Shit, Gus. Do I need to spell it out for you? Okay. The answer is yes. I think I'm falling in love with you. There. I've said it. And before you give *me* a hard time for the lecture I gave *you* about not falling in love with your first—just disregard all of that. I was wrong."

Gus smiled, looked down, and shook his head. "I already did," he said, gazing back at Sam. "Like it or not, I'm pretty sure you're officially my first love."

Sam smiled broadly. "Well, imagine that," he said. "Now that we have that out in the open, we can figure out where to go from here. It won't be easy, but we'll make it work."

Before Gus could answer, they both looked up at the sound of squealing tires. "Oh jeez," Gus said, recognizing his mother's Mercedes. "I think our ride is here."

Chapter Fifteen
A Garden Party

THE NOONDAY sun filled the room as Gus stepped up to the mirror. "How do I look?" he asked, situating his cover on his head and staring at his reflection.

Sam glanced at the back of the door out of habit as he slipped his coat over his shoulders. "Good enough to eat," he said softly, crossing the room and slipping his arms around Gus's waist.

They were a little more relaxed behind the locked bedroom door, but still very cautious.

It had been Gus's bright idea to keep the door locked behind them, and if someone questioned it, he could always say he must have hit the lock by accident when he'd closed it. So far so good. No one had even tried the doorknob or knocked.

Gus closed his eyes, laid his hand on top of Sam's, and squeezed. "You're nothing but a big ole tease."

"We'll see how much of a tease I am tomorrow," Sam said, tightening his grip.

"Last night was torture," Gus admitted. "Being away from campus and still not being able to be ourselves."

"Yeah, but it was sure nice sharing a bed for a little while," Sam added.

After the family dinner and a cognac with Gus's father, which had gone remarkably well, Sam and Gus had retired. Gus locked the door behind them, but neither of them felt comfortable attempting anything remotely resembling sex while Gus's parents were still at home. So they crawled into Gus's twin bed and made out a little, but mostly held and caressed each other, something they hadn't experienced before.

Gus turned around in Sam's arms and took a small step back. He started buttoning the gold buttons on Sam's white coat. "It *was* great to hold you, but God that was surely a test of my will," Gus said. "So tough to be that close to you and not take it any further."

Sam smiled. "It looks like someone I know has totally gotten over his nerves regarding his first time."

Gus brushed Sam's lips lightly with his and moved his mouth to Sam's ear. "I am so ready, I'm gonna eat you alive tomorrow."

The meaning behind Gus's words and the man's hot breath against his ear sent shivers down Sam's spine, which in turn sent the blood rushing to his groin. "Fuck, Gus. If you don't stop that shit, I'm gonna have to escort your mom to her table with a raging hard-on. How's that gonna look in my dress whites?"

"Pretty damn hot if you ask me."

"You're not helping," Sam said.

Gus's hand was heading for his crotch to steal a grope when they heard a gentle knock on the door. The two men instinctively stepped apart. "Boys," Gus's mother said, "it's time."

Gus gave Sam a quick peck on the cheek and walked over to the door. When he opened it, his mother stepped inside in a flowing peach-colored dress that came down right below her knees. All Sam could think of was the reruns of *Dynasty* his mother had watched over and over again. Gus's mother looked just like Alexis Carrington Colby.

The woman was stunning all right, but she looked like a major diva ready for a garden party.

"You look beautiful, Mom," Gus said. Gus looked at Sam and cleared his throat.

Oh shit! "Ah, yes, Mrs. McRae, Gus is right. You do look beautiful."

Anne-Emerson Beaufort McRae glowed from their compliments. "Thank you, boys. And you both look so handsome." Anne-Emerson kissed Gus on the cheek. She held her hands out in Sam's direction, and he took them into his. "Stewart—oh, I mean, Sam. We are so glad to have you here and honored that you would allow us to be your family away from home. This is gonna be so much fun."

Sam tried to think of something appropriate to say, but he had no clue. This was all so new to him. He finally said, "Thank you, Mrs. McRae. It's my honor." *There. That was okay. I think.*

Anne-Emerson nodded. "Well, boys? Are you ready to escort this lady to a garden party?"

"Yes, ma'am," they said in unison.

Gus removed his cover, tucked it under his left arm, and offered his right to his mother. Sam reached for his cover on the bed and did as Gus had, and the three of them walked down the massive staircase to the backyard.

When they got to the back of the house, Mrs. McRae stopped and stood in the doorway while Gus and Sam situated their covers. Sam looked out onto the garden, and he couldn't believe his eyes. It looked like another scene right out of *Dynasty*.

The lawn was covered with skirted tables, all perfectly set with china and crystal. A string quartet was playing soft classical music, and servers in black tie were milling about serving champagne and hors d'oeuvres from silver trays. And that was just what he could see from his current vantage point.

All the men were dressed in seersucker suits or navy blue blazers with khaki pants, sporting bowties, and with what Gus had described as white bucks on their feet. The women were dressed in various colorful dresses and dripping with their finest jewelry. Sam felt like Alice from *Alice in Wonderland*, and he hadn't even stepped out of the house yet. The music stopped and Gus's father joined them in the doorway. He tapped a knife against his glass and cleared his throat.

"Ladies and gentlemen, I'd like to introduce my wife and your hostess for the afternoon, Anne-Emerson Beaufort McRae, and our guests of honor, Citadel Cadets Angus Conrad McRae the third and Stewart Adam Morley."

"Here we go, boys," Mrs. McRae said. The music started again, and Gus and Sam lifted their covers to their heads as Mrs. McRae took a step forward. Gus and Sam followed, and the three of them walked down a makeshift aisle, Gus's mother smiling and nodding her head in each direction and Gus and Sam looking straight ahead as if they were marching in formation.

When they reached Mrs. McRae's table, she took her seat, and the music stopped once again. Sam and Gus did an about-face, removed their covers, and stood at ease. Gus looked at Sam and smiled. Sam was literally weak in the knees at how handsome Gus looked in his dress whites, but he did his best to mask his awe and admiration as Gus began to speak.

"Cadet Morley and I would like to thank you and my parents for honoring us in this way. We feel extremely privileged to be attending the Citadel and blessed to have your continued support throughout our journey. All we can say is thank you."

The music started once more, and Sam felt a smile spread across his face when Gus winked at him and offered his hand. The two cadets shook, and it was as though everyone disappeared except the two of them. Sam knew in reality it was only a second, but it felt like an eternity as he and Gus gazed into each other's eyes.

Everyone applauded, bringing Sam out of his daze, and Gus released his hand, threw his arm over Sam's shoulder, and whispered in his ear, "Thank God that shit's over with. Let's eat."

Sam nodded. "You did a great job, by the way."

"Thanks."

"Oh!" Sam added. "Please promise me you won't leave me alone too often. I don't want to be rude, but I have nothing in common with any of these people."

"I promise."

About an hour later, Gus got up from the table and went to the bar to get them each a beer. Sam followed Gus's movements and wondered how this all came to be. "What are the odds," he whispered to himself. *Two gay guys from very different backgrounds in an all-straight military college get thrown together in the same barracks, have a rocky start, and then decide to try and make a go of it. It's just crazy!*

Sam was still watching Gus at the bar, waiting for their beers, when Gus turned and their eyes locked. Again, it was as though everyone disappeared except the two of them. He could see and almost feel the caring and desire in Gus's eyes. The blood rushed right back to his groin, and he knew there would be no getting up for at least ten minutes. Gus held his gaze until the bartender handed him the beers and he started back in Sam's direction.

Gus set Sam's beer down on the table, leaned in close, and whispered into his ear. "Please tell me you felt that?"

"Hell yeah," Sam said. "Every bit of it. Tomorrow can't come soon enough for me."

The party went on until almost nine o'clock. Mr. and Mrs. McRae, along with Emmy, Gus, and Sam, stood at the large wrought-iron gate, saying good-bye to everyone as they departed. By the time the last guest disappeared down the driveway, Sam's back ached, and his feet were killing him.

"As usual I think everything was just lovely, darlin'," Mr. McRae said to his wife.

"It was," Sam agreed. "Thank you both so very much for including me."

Mr. McRae nodded. "It was our pleasure, son."

Mrs. McRae kissed Sam and Gus on the cheek. "We were happy to do it. Now you boys go on upstairs and get comfortable. Leave your uniforms on the bathroom floor, and I'll have Mary take them to the dry cleaners and make sure to have them back by the end of the week."

"Yes, ma'am," Gus said, hugging his mother. Although he knew this party was as much for his parents' standing in the community as it was for him and Sam, his parents were who they were and that was never going to change. So he offered a kind word. "As Sam said, thanks. It was very nice of you to do this."

Anne-Emerson smiled. "We're proud of you both. Now go on up and relax."

"MY FEET are killing me," Sam said as he and Gus walked up the stairs.

"Mine too," Gus agreed. "Maybe I can do a little something to help in that department."

Gus opened his bedroom door and held it for Sam, took his cover from him, and tossed it onto the bed along with his. He locked the door behind them, walked over in front of Sam, and started unbuttoning his coat.

"I could get used to this," Sam said.

Gus chuckled. "Don't get too used to it. We only have a week off. Then it's back to limited touching."

Gus slid Sam's white coat over his shoulders and tossed it to the other bed next to the hats. He ran his hands over Sam's soft white T-shirt, which was warm and smelled just like Sam. Gus kissed Sam gently and started backing him up toward the bed until Sam stopped. One firm push had Sam flat on his back in the middle of the bed.

Gus removed his own coat and added it to the pile. By now Sam was sitting up and leaning against the headboard. Gus toed off his shoes and sat cross-legged on the end of the bed. He took Sam's left foot into his lap, untied the shiny black shoe, and slipped it off.

Sam wiggled his toes and sighed as the shoe hit the floor with a thud.

Gus removed Sam's other shoe and took both of Sam's feet in his hands. He started rubbing and kneading, paying special attention to Sam's arches and the balls of his feet.

"God, Gus! That feels so good."

Gus watched Sam's facial expressions as they went from exhaustion to relaxation in no time at all. When Sam closed his eyes, Gus knew he was doing something right. Gus took this time to really study Sam. He'd secretly watched him sleep before, but something was different now. He'd always been handsome, but at that moment Sam was the most gorgeous man he'd ever seen. He stared in awe at his handsome cadet and blessed his good fortune.

Minutes later Sam's eyes flew open, and his face contorted into a surprised expression. "I'm sorry, Gus. I think I fell asleep."

"Shhh," Gus said. "You did, and it's okay. That means you were relaxed."

"Stretch out and let me return the favor."

Gus did as bid, and Sam took his feet into his lap.

"You're right," Gus said with a happy sigh. "That does feel good."

Sam smiled. "I'm glad."

"I sure wish Rav could have been here today," Gus said.

"Me too. But she has a girlfriend now. And it was a big weekend for her, meeting Valerie's parents for the first time."

"I'll bet she was scared shitless."

"Me too. I hope it all went well."

"Sam?"

"Yeah?"

"Thank you for putting up with all of this today."

"No problem," Sam said. "My mother taught me to be gracious, and it was very nice of your parents, whatever their reasons, to do this for us."

In a move that surprised even him, Gus dug his foot into Sam's crotch and started rubbing. Sam was still massaging the other foot, but he leaned his head back and closed his eyes. Gus could feel Sam's erection growing, which in turn was getting him very excited.

"Just one more night," Sam said.

Gus jumped and hopped off the bed when a knock sounded. He threw Sam's cover and coat onto his own bed and went for the door.

When he opened it, his father was standing on the other side. "Hey, Dad."

"Everything okay in here?"

"Yes, sir. We were just resting."

"Oh. Sorry to bother. You boys turning in?"

"If you don't mind, I think we will. We're both really tired and looking forward to a good night's sleep."

"I remember my Knob days, and I totally understand. Good night, cadets."

"Good night and thanks again."

Angus nodded and turned.

Gus closed the door and engaged the lock. He checked the door to make sure it was secure and sighed.

Gus walked over to Sam's bed, pulling his T-shirt over his head as he went. He removed his socks and released his pants, letting them drop to the floor. Gus offered Sam his hands. When Sam accepted, Gus pulled him to his feet and buried his face in Sam's neck.

"I don't think I can wait until tomorrow. I want you so badly it hurts."

"I know," Sam said. "I feel the same way, but we've got to. We're disciplined cadets. We can do this."

Gus took a step back, pulled Sam's T-shirt over his head, and tossed it to the floor. Next, he got to work on his pants. When they were down around Sam's ankles, Gus dropped to his knees as Sam stepped out of them. He lifted Sam's feet, removed his socks, and then glanced up for a moment. Then he buried his face in Sam's crotch, mimicking what Sam had done to him back in their dorm room by wrapping his mouth around Sam's length through his underwear.

Sam squeezed Gus's shoulders and a gasp escaped Sam's lips. "Please, stop," Sam whispered, gripping Gus under his armpits and pulling him up, "or I won't be able to."

Sam cupped the back of Gus's neck, plastered his lips over Gus's mouth, and ground his crotch into Gus's. He slid his tongue into Gus's mouth and their tongues roamed freely while they bumped and ground against each other.

"We've got to stop," Sam said, breaking the kiss. "We can do this, Gus. Just one more day."

Gus dropped his head and led Sam to his bed. He pulled back the covers and slid in, patting the spot next to him. "Come on," he whispered. "Just for a little while. Besides, the sooner we go to sleep, the sooner it will be tomorrow."

CHAPTER SIXTEEN
ALONE AT LAST

WHEN GUS opened his eyes, he blinked against the bright morning sunlight flooding the room. He instinctively tightened his grip on Sam and then almost instantly panicked. Sam was still in his arms, sleeping like a baby. *Oh fuck, we slept like this all night!*

His first inclination was to jump out of bed, but his body wouldn't move. He didn't want to move. *Fuck it! We're fine.* No one had knocked on the door. All was well. He closed his eyes again and kissed the top of Sam's head. Sam stirred, snuggling in a little closer, but he didn't wake up. *Our second morning waking up together. Well, technically Sam is still asleep, but at least we're in the same bed.*

Gus looked over at the alarm clock. *Shit!*

"Sam?" he said quietly, rubbing the top of Sam's head. "We've got to get up. It's almost ten."

Sam moaned and snuggled a little closer to Gus. Gus smiled and tightened his grip again. Then Sam sat bolt upright in bed and looked around. "Fuck! We slept like this all night."

Gus smiled and nodded. "Yeah. But we're okay."

Sam looked at the door out of habit and then lay back down in Gus's arms. "Shit, Gus," he whispered. "We can't let this happen at the Citadel."

"It won't. I promise. We won't be stupid enough to get in the same bed."

"You're right," Sam said, backing up to Gus and pulling Gus's hand around his waist. "But damn this feels so good."

"It does. It's been years since I've slept through the night."

"It's been years since I've slept in the same bed with anyone," Sam added. "Let alone through the night."

"But you do know we're gonna have to get up. My parents will be leaving shortly, and we need to say good-bye."

"I know," Sam whined.

"But look on the bright side. As soon as they're gone, we get the place to ourselves."

Sam threw Gus's hand off him and jumped out of the bed. "Well, let's go. Maybe they're waiting for us to say good-bye."

Sam disappeared into the bathroom, and then the toilet flushed and the faucet came on. Thirty seconds later, Sam stuck his head out of the door with a white foamy mouth, moving a toothbrush vigorously. "Ca–mon. Gut–up. Wa—au–u–waying–fa?"

"What?"

Instead of repeating himself, Sam made a motion for Gus to join him in the bathroom. Gus hopped out of bed, and when he entered the bathroom, Sam was rinsing his mouth.

"What was that all about?" Gus asked.

"I said, 'Come on. Get up. What are you waiting for?'"

"Really?"

"Yes," Sam teased. "Don't you understand English?"

"Yeah! But that wasn't English."

Gus relieved himself and brushed his teeth. When he got back to the bedroom, Sam had messed up the other bed. He winked at Gus. "Just to be on the safe side."

"Good thinking," Gus said, digging through his dresser. He tossed Sam a pair of shorts and a T-shirt and retrieved the same for himself. "Let's go move them along."

Gus and Sam rounded the stairs to find Emmy sitting on the last step, her bags at the front door. She looked up at the sound of footsteps. "Morning, sleeping beauties."

"Morning," Gus and Sam said in unison.

Gus kissed the top of her head. "All packed and ready to go?"

"Of course," Emmy mumbled. "Dad said to be ready by ten, but as usual he must have forgot to tell Mom. So here I sit."

"Don't be fresh, young lady," Angus the elder said, walking into the foyer with a cup of coffee. "Your mother will be down shortly."

Emmy rolled her eyes. "Yes, sir."

"Mornin', boys," Angus said. "Sleep well?"

"Really well," Gus answered, looking at Sam and trying to hide a smile.

"Yes, sir," Sam said. "Very comfortable bed."

"Glad to hear it." Angus chuckled to himself and shook his head. "I do remember how uncomfortable those bunks are over at the Citadel." He glanced at his watch. "Jesus! Look at the time. Anne-Emerson," he yelled up the stairs. "We need to get a move on."

He looked at the boys again. "Cocktails are at five. It's a three plus hour drive, and you know how long it takes these two beauties to get ready."

"Yes, sir," Gus said. "I remember."

"Ha-ha," Emmy said. "That's very funny, Dad."

"Coming," Gus's mother called from the top of the stairs. "Will one of you boys help me with my overnight bag?"

"Yes, ma'am," Sam said, taking the stairs two at a time. He took Mrs. McRae's bag from her and carried it to the front door.

"Thank you, Sam," she said, smiling. "I think I finally have that name down."

"Thank you," Sam said.

Gus and Sam loaded all the bags into the car and waited. "Are you sure you boys are going to be okay?"

"We'll be fine, Mom," Gus said.

"Today's Mary's day off, but there's food in the fridge if you boys get hungry."

"Thank you, Mrs. McRae," Sam said.

"Now, Angus," Mr. McRae said. "When we get back, I want to have a long talk about your future."

Gus stiffened. "Dad! We're having a really nice stay. Do you really think we should go and ruin it by discussing topics we don't agree on?"

"Oh, Angus," Anne-Emerson said. "The boy's right. Can't we just have a pleasant Thanksgiving break?"

"Fine," Angus said. "But we're going to have to discuss it sooner or later."

"Thanks, Mom. And Dad, we'll discuss it when you decide you're gonna allow me to make my own career choices."

Angus opened his mouth, apparently to object, but Anne-Emerson interrupted. "Now, now, you two. Let's go, Angus, or we're gonna be late."

Angus huffed and got in the car without another word. "Thanks," Gus mouthed to his mother. She nodded and got in the car. She rolled down the window. "Have fun, boys."

"Oh, we will," Gus said, winking at Sam.

The Mercedes drove away, leaving Sam and Gus standing on the edge of the circular driveway. "My father takes every opportunity he can to ruin a moment and piss me off."

"I've got something to take your mind off of your father," Sam said, waving his arm toward the door and gesturing for Gus to go ahead of him.

Gus smiled. "I'll bet you do."

Gus held the front door for Sam, and when Sam entered, he slammed the door closed and turned the deadbolt. He looked out of the sidelights to make sure his parents were really gone, and when he turned, Sam was sitting on the stairs, watching him. Gus lunged forward and landed on top of Sam, cupped his face, and kissed him deeply.

"If the stairs weren't so visible from the front door, I'd take you right here."

Sam laughed. "Are you sure you haven't done this before?"

"Only in my mind," Gus said. "I've had a lot of time to imagine what I was going to do to you, and thank God, the time has come."

Sam stood and took Gus by the hand. When they reached the bedroom, Sam locked the door behind them for double security and led Gus to the bed. "Are you sure?" Sam asked.

"Never been more sure of anything in my life," Gus whispered.

Sam pulled Gus close to him, and when their lips met, it was as though Sam had opened the door to a lifetime of imprisoned passion. Gus's hands were frantically roaming over every inch of Sam's body, pulling him as close as humanly possible. Sam felt different to him now. Unbridled and free, and Gus loved the way he felt in Sam's arms.

Suddenly Sam started panting almost uncontrollably. He rested his forehead against Gus's. "Jesus, Gus, stop."

Gus froze. "Wait! No! Why? Am I doing something wrong?"

"Fuck no! You're doing everything right. And because of it, I'm about to come in my shorts. We just need to slow down."

Gus smiled with relief. "God, I thought I was fucking this up."

Sam kissed him gently on the lips and smiled. "No fucking way you can screw this up. You're perfect."

"So are you," Gus said, taking a deep breath. "Okay. You wanna try this again? A little slower this time?"

"Oh yeah," Sam said, gripping the hem of Gus's T-shirt and pulling it up to Gus's chest. Gus lifted his arms and the shirt came off and went flying across the room.

Gus didn't close his eyes for fear this encounter was all a dream. And if it was a dream, it would become a nightmare quickly if he woke up before he saw it to an end. He put his hands on Sam's shoulders to steady himself and focused only on Sam.

When Sam ran his hands over Gus's chest, Gus shivered in anticipation. Sam brushed over his nipples with his thumbs, and Gus closed his eyes at the odd but wonderful sensation. Sam's hands suddenly slid down to Gus's waist and rested on his thighs. Sam stood on his tiptoes and pressed his lips against Gus's for a long, wet kiss. He then kissed his way down Gus's neck, shoulders, and chest until he covered one of Gus's nipples with his mouth.

The warm, wet sensation was delicious, and when Sam bit down lightly on his nipple, Gus sucked in a ragged breath, and his cock twitched in his shorts. Without conscious volition, one of his hands went to the back of Sam's head and pulled him tighter against Gus's chest, and the other hand cupped Sam's ass, lifting Sam off the ground. Gus carried Sam to the foot of the bed, and Sam ended up on his back with Gus on top of him.

"I like this position," Sam said.

"Meeee too."

Lifting up a bit, Sam pulled his T-shirt over his head, exposing his broad muscular chest. Although Gus had seen it many times, it was almost like he was looking at it for the first time. This time, Sam's chest was his to explore. His to lick and tease and even bite if he wanted to. The options were endless, and in Gus's mind he pictured exactly what he was going to do. Being a twenty-year-old virgin gave a person a lot of time to think about their first time, and although he might not have physically done it before, he'd seen enough to know exactly what he was going to do. *I want Sam, and I want him now. No more waiting.*

Sliding to Sam's left side, Gus rested his knee across Sam's torso and worked it slowly up and down over Sam's erection. He moved his arm under Sam's neck and ran his hand over the smoothly shaved head, turning Sam's face to his. When their eyes met, Gus plastered his lips to Sam's in a deep, wet kiss.

As their tongues thrashed, Gus slid his left hand down, down Sam's chest, over his torso, and without so much as a pause for thought, right into the waistband of his shorts. He gingerly took Sam's erection into his hand, and when he squeezed, he felt as much as heard Sam gasp into their kiss.

It was an odd sensation having his fingers wrapped around a cock other than his own, but exhilarating at the same time. If he had to guess, he was a little longer than Sam, but Sam was definitely a bit thicker than he was. Gus moved his hand up and down Sam's length, and Sam moved his hips in unison with Gus's strokes.

"Jesus," Sam whispered against Gus's open mouth. "I thought I was the one teaching you."

Gus smiled against Sam's lips. "You are. I'm flying by the seat of my pants here."

"Then you're a natural born pilot," Sam said. "You're doing great."

That was all the encouragement Gus needed. He slid down to the foot of the bed, pulled Sam's shorts and underwear down and off, and tossed them to the side. "Now I've got what I want."

Gus positioned himself between Sam's legs and ran his hands up and down Sam's thighs. Without a moment's hesitation, he leaned forward and took Sam into his mouth. Sam arched his back and cried out Gus's name, which only gave him more confidence.

Gus had experienced Sam's unique scent on his skin and on his clothing, but it was so much heavier and more pronounced in his groin area. Wanting more, he slid his mouth all the way down Sam's length. At first Gus fought his gag reflex, but then he relaxed his throat, buried his nose in Sam's pubic hair, and inhaled deeply. The scent was an aphrodisiac, and it was driving him wild.

Sam's cock was warm and hard, and his skin was as soft as anything he'd ever imagined. Gus wasn't sure what he'd been expecting, but this was so much better than anything he could have conjured up in his mind.

Sam's hand rested lightly on Gus's head, and he moaned and thrust his hips up in unison with Gus's movements.

Gus was just getting into a rhythm when, in a move that surprised the hell out of him, Sam was up on his knees, repositioning him. Before Gus knew it, he was on his back and looking up at Sam's smiling face.

"Damn," Gus said. "That was smooth."

Sam winked. "And talking about smooth moves," he said, "are you sure you haven't given a blowjob before?"

"I swear," Gus said.

"Again, you're a natural."

In another unexpected move, Gus's shorts and underwear were down his legs and over his ankles.

Feeling a little exposed and vulnerable, Gus lay there naked with his erection pointing north and Sam smiling down at him. But he trusted Sam, and he wanted this. Badly.

The second Sam stretched out on top of him, Gus's insecurities were a thing of the past. Their lips met again, and Sam ground his erection into Gus's. Gus wrapped his arms around Sam's neck and his legs around Sam's back, then locked his ankles, holding Sam in place as if he were going to try to get away. Together they rocked back and forth. The sensation of Sam's cock against his almost brought Gus to the end.

"Stop, Sam! I'm so close." Sam stopped moving, and Gus unlocked his ankles and dropped his legs.

Gus tried to catch his breath as Sam kissed his way down his chest and stomach, but he cried out when Sam swallowed him all the way to the back of his throat. Gus fisted the sheets when Sam slid up to the tip and then swallowed him again.

"Sam! Nooo," he cried.

But it was no use. What Sam was doing felt so incredible, Gus had no power to stop him.

Sam continued to move up and down in a slow, steady motion, bringing Gus closer and closer to his release with each move. Seconds later, Gus thrust his hips forward, arched his back, and cried out

Sam's name as a whole new universe opened up to him and he came. He rode out the pleasure as Sam moved effortlessly with each thrust. When Sam finally released him, Gus felt like he'd run a marathon. And won.

Sam looked up at him and smiled. He inched his way up and kissed Gus. Gus could taste his own release on Sam's tongue, and it was oddly erotic. He smacked Sam on the top of the head playfully.

"What was that for?" Sam asked.

"Making me come so soon."

"It's called taking the edge off," Sam explained. "We have all day and all night to do this. The next time will be slow and easy."

"But wait!" Gus said. "What about you?"

"Too late," Sam said, holding up his right hand dripping with come. "You were so beautiful when you came, I couldn't help myself."

Gus smiled. "Thank you."

"For what?"

"Being my first."

"Well," Sam said. "If I have anything to say about it, I'm gonna be your first, second, third, and fourth. And that's just today."

CHAPTER SEVENTEEN
SAM AND GUS

SAM AND Gus spent the entire day taking turns pleasuring each other. Sam loved how with each round, he learned a little more about what made Gus moan or cry out, and he did his best to hit all those hot spots as often as possible.

Sam hadn't really considered himself an attentive lover, but with Gus he really wanted to be. Gus made it so hard not to be. The way he looked at Sam with such adoration. The way he threw his head back, closed his eyes, and called out Sam's name each time he came. It nearly drove Sam wild.

And Gus had proved to be a very quick study. He was a gentle lover—and rough at the same time. He gave more than he took, and it seemed like his greatest pleasure was pleasuring Sam.

When seven thirty rolled around, they were still in bed, Sam was leaning back against the headboard, and Gus was lying next to him, his head resting on Sam's chest while he drew little circles on Sam's stomach.

"Something on your mind you wanna share?" Sam asked.

"I don't know. I'm thinking."

"About what?"

"The Citadel."

"What about it?"

"I don't know if I can go back now."

"I know what you mean."

"Why can't we just leave?" Gus said, looking up at Sam. "We can go someplace where it's just the two of us."

"That's a great idea, but how will we survive?"

"Fuck!" Gus said. "I don't know. I mean I know we have to go back, but it's gonna be so hard."

"Okay," Sam said. "Let's look at the positives."

"You mean there are positives?"

"Of course there are positives. For starters, we get to go back together. That's more than some couples get. Yeah, we can't have sex, but we get to share a room. We'll see each other every day."

"I guess when you put it that way," Gus said. "But the sex part really sucks."

"I know, but we get Christmas break in a little over a month. We can hold out until then."

Gus looked up again. "Is it gonna be that easy for you?"

Sam kissed Gus's forehead. "Hell no! But we have no other choice. I'd rather be thankful for what we have instead of bitching about what we don't have."

Gus sighed. "You're right. I'm acting like that spoiled rich kid you thought I was."

Sam chuckled. "Maybe a little."

"I'm sorry. It's just...." Gus's voice trailed off.

"Just what?"

Gus hesitated. "Sam. I know I shouldn't say this, but I think I'm falling in love with you, and not being able to touch you or hold you or make love to you is going to be tough."

Sam reached down, slipped his finger under Gus's chin, and tilted his head back. "I feel the same way, Gus, and I know it's gonna be tough, but at least we'll be together. Imagine if we had to go off to different schools."

Gus craned his neck and kissed Sam on the cheek. "You're right. I'm being a baby. We'll make it work."

"I'm hungry," Sam said.

"Me too. Why don't we shower and then go downstairs and see what's in the fridge?"

"Sounds good to me."

AN HOUR later Gus and Sam were pawing at each other and kissing their way back up the main staircase, not caring if God or the neighbors got a pornographic show. It had started all over again when they were eating halibut, mashed potatoes, and steamed veggies left over from the garden party, and Sam had dropped a forkful of mashed potatoes in his lap. Gus had decided it might be a good idea to lick Sam's shorts clean instead of using a towel. One thing led to another, and soon they were pawing at each other and heading back upstairs.

While Gus had been licking his shorts clean and giving him an impromptu blowjob at the breakfast bar, Sam had decided it was time to take their relationship one step further. He had no idea when they were going to get the chance to be together like this again. Probably not until Christmas break, and he wanted a stronger connection. Something to get him through the long Citadel nights. Sam knew he wanted Gus in every way before they went back to school, and although he'd been thoroughly satisfied with what they had done all day, now he had an itch that needed scratching, and he had no idea how Gus was going to feel about it. *You'll never know if you don't ask, Sammy boy!*

As they made their way up the stairs, Gus was undressing Sam little by little, and by the time they reached the bedroom, Sam was naked and Gus was working on himself. It turned out the rookie had an insatiable appetite for lovemaking, and Sam was thrilled about that.

Completely naked now and rolling around on the bed, hot and heavy, Sam finally got the courage to broach the subject. "Gus," he whispered between kisses.

"Yeah?"

"You trust me, right?"

"You know I do," Gus said, stopping midkiss and studying him warily. "Why?"

"Because I have a couple more things to introduce you to. You game?"

The concern on Gus's face morphed into a smile. "Hell yeah!"

That's all Sam needed to hear. In one of his flash maneuvers, he had Gus's legs up over his head and was looking at his ass.

"Whoa!" Gus said, squirming a little but eventually relinquishing control. "Shit, this is weird."

"It's okay," Sam said. "You're gonna really enjoy this."

"IF YOU say—" was all Gus got out before something wet and slightly rough went where nothing like it had ever gone before.

"Damn!" he hissed, moving his ass back and forth, enjoying the warm but strange sensation.

"Jesus, Sam! What are you doing to me?"

Sam stopped licking long enough to say, "It's called a rim job." Then he sank his tongue into Gus's ass again.

Gus gyrated uncontrollably. He and his ass were in heaven, and there was no denying it. As Sam held his cheeks apart, teasing, licking, and circling the sensitive skin just inside and outside his opening, Gus's ass was literally tingling. It was like a thousand nerve endings were being massaged. He'd stuck a finger up there a time or two, like every adolescent, but it had never been like this.

Gus fisted the sheets and arched his back when Sam took his cock into his hand and stroked in unison with his licking and probing.

"Holy shit," Gus said, thrusting his hips forward into Sam's grip while Sam's tongue teased and licked his ass. The two sensations were so different but connected in some way. The way his ass was tied to his dick was almost too much to handle. He was enjoying everything about this and wanted it to go on forever, but he also wanted Sam to feel the same pleasure.

"Sam," Gus whispered. "Can I try this on you?"

"I thought you'd never ask," Sam teased.

Sam took one last lick, lowered Gus's legs, and smiled up at him. Gus pushed himself up on his hands and got to his knees. He nudged Sam onto his back and lifted Sam's legs as Sam had done his.

Gus was mesmerized. He'd never seen another person's opening that closely, except while watching porn, and after examining it, he suddenly had the desire to be balls deep inside of it. But first things first. He pulled Sam's asscheeks apart and made the initial pass with his tongue. The aroma was all Sam, and the taste was sweet on the tip of his tongue. Sam's opening quivered a little and then relaxed. Gus touched the opening with his finger, and it quivered again, and with that quiver came a moan from Sam. The sound of Sam's moan shot straight to Gus's dick, and he wanted more than ever to be inside Sam. The anticipation of the possibility propelled him forward, and he dove in face-first, licking and tantalizing Sam's ass, coaxing sounds from Sam he'd never heard before. Sam was now gyrating like Gus had been, and that, too, encouraged him to continue with the gentle assault.

"Gus," Sam said hesitantly.

Gus stopped and looked up between Sam's legs. "Am I doing something wrong?"

"Exactly the opposite. You're doing everything right, but I want more."

That was exactly what Gus had been hoping for. Before he could voice the thought, though, Sam spoke again. "I want you inside me."

"God! I want that too," Gus whispered. "But I've never...."

"I'll show you everything. Do you have lube and condoms?"

"No condoms, but I have lotion. Do we really need condoms?"

"I don't think so," Sam said. "I haven't been with anyone since my Citadel physical six months ago. Lord knows I was tested for HIV and everything under the sun."

"I had the same physical, and since you're my first, I think we're safe."

"Okay, then," Sam said. "Where's the lotion?"

"In the bathroom. Drawer to the right of the sink."

When Sam returned, Gus was sporting a raging erection and a wicked grin. "This is so hot."

"So you're good with this?"

"Hell yeah! A little nervous. I mean... I want to do this right. But I trust you and will follow your lead."

Sam nodded. "I think we should start with me on top."

Gus stretched out on the bed, squeezed and held up his erection. "He's ready and waiting, cadet."

Sam couldn't hold back his laughter. "Sure didn't take you long to get used to all of this."

"Like I told you, it has happened a thousand times in my mind."

Climbing back on the bed, Sam straddled Gus's legs. He leaned forward and took Gus into his mouth, all the way to the back of his throat.

Gus hissed, threw his head back, and looked at Sam. "I don't ever think I'll get used to how good that feels."

"Let's hope you don't," Sam said, flipping the top of the bottle and squeezing a little lotion into his hand. He reached around and lubricated his opening, squeezed more out and warmed it in his hands before coating himself and Gus, moving his hand up and down.

Gus locked his fingers behind his head and watched Sam closely. "That feels incredible," he said.

"If you think that feels good, just wait."

"Enough with the promises," Gus teased. "Let's see some action."

Sam laughed again. "Patience, my little cadet. Patience."

Sam rose up to his knees and shimmied up Gus's torso.

In anticipation, Gus unlocked his hands from behind his head and rested them on Sam's thighs. He watched in awe as his handsome man positioned himself over his groin and then slowly lowered himself, a little at first and then more and more, until he was completely seated. Gus squeezed Sam's thighs, and his eyes rolled into his head as Sam's warm, tight heat surrounded him.

When Gus regained a semblance of control and opened his eyes, it was to the most beautiful thing he'd ever seen. Sam's head was thrown back, and he was wearing an expression of pure pleasure on his face.

Then he looked down at Gus. "You okay?"

"Better than okay," Gus said. "This feels great, and you are a beautiful man."

"Here we go, then." Sam started to move. He lifted up slowly and slid back down again, reseating himself, and then he repeated the action over and over again, slowly and deliberately.

Gus moved his hands to Sam's waist and followed his up and down movements. The sensation of Sam's tight heat encircling him was like no other feeling. His own hand had never even come close, and the fact that it was Sam doing this to him, giving him such pleasure, made it all even more special.

Sam leaned forward and covered Gus's lips with his own as he continued to move. Gus thrust his hips up to meet Sam's motions, and Sam began to moan against his mouth. "God, Gus! You feel so good."

Gus smiled against Sam's lips. "Just don't stop. Ever!"

"I want you on top of me," Sam said.

"Hold on, and don't move," Gus said as he maneuvered his body without unseating Sam. He slid to the end of the bed, put his feet on the floor, grabbed Sam under his ass, and lifted him right off the bed. Gus turned around, still standing, and gently laid Sam on his back. He raised Sam's legs, rested them on his shoulders, and smiled down at him.

"How was that?"

"Like a pro," Sam said. "Now move!"

Gus did as he was told, gingerly at first and then a little faster. When a slight moan issued from Sam's mouth and Sam fisted the sheets, Gus almost lost control. He picked up speed, pulling almost all the way out and then pushing forward again as far as he could go. For some reason he couldn't get deep enough, close enough, to Sam to suit his needs. Between Sam's groans, whines, whimpers, the occasional "Oh God" and "Jesus," and Sam calling his name, Gus hoped he was doing everything right.

Instinct must have taken over, because Gus was no longer in control of his own actions. He grabbed Sam's feet by the ankles and held his legs open as he plowed in and out of him. He moved one leg over the other, turning Sam almost onto his side, which gave him even better access. With that move, Gus's name escaped Sam's lips again… and again. But this time the tone was pleading, and it drove Gus mad with desire.

Sam opened his eyes and looked up at Gus. He wore such an expression of love and adoration, Gus almost came right then. Sam took Gus's hands and pulled him closer, but when Gus leaned forward, his angle wasn't right and he slipped out. Sam scooted up to the head of the bed and motioned for Gus to join him. He turned over onto his stomach and brought his left knee forward, giving Gus clear access. Gus seated himself behind Sam and slowly pushed his way in. He felt Sam stiffen briefly and then relax. Gus started to move again, kissing Sam's back and shoulders until Sam threw his left leg over Gus and twisted his head so they were now face to face. Gus thrust his hips forward as he covered Sam's lips in a wet, crushing kiss.

To Gus, this was the best position yet. Like this, he and Sam fit together like hand and glove. Gus had the perfect angle, giving him the best access, and he was still able to have Sam in his arms while he kissed him passionately.

With each thrust Sam moaned into Gus's kiss. Gus's balls tightened as his imminent release grew closer. He wanted them to come together, as one, so he took Sam's length into his left hand, amazed at how hard Sam was. He stroked Sam's cock in time with his thrusts, and Sam whimpered against his mouth.

"Oh, Gus, I'm so close."

"Me too," Gus said, his heart racing and his actions now becoming more frantic. He was pumping faster and harder than he could have ever imagined, and Sam was taking it all and seemed to be loving it. Sam suddenly stiffened in his arms, wailed against his mouth, and shot the first round of his release while Gus plowed into him over and over.

Sam's first shot covered his own chest and stomach and Gus's hand. Watching Sam sent Gus over the top, and he shot the first round of his load deep inside his lover. With each thrust Sam released more of his load, spurt after spurt, again and again, until he convulsed and nothing more came out. Gus simultaneously continued to empty his balls until there was nothing left, and the two men collapsed into each other's arms.

Gus didn't move an inch for fear of becoming dislodged. He wanted to stay deep inside of Sam for as long as he could. Sam didn't seem to want to move either, so they stayed that way, their arms wrapped tightly around each other, their foreheads touching as they gasped and fought to catch their breath. Unfortunately, the inevitable happened, and Gus eventually slipped from Sam to both of their moans of disapproval.

Gus got up long enough to get a warm cloth from the bathroom. He cleaned Sam and then himself, then climbed back into bed, pulled the covers up over them, and wrapped his arms around Sam. "That was the most incredible thing I have ever done," Gus said when he could finally find the words.

Sam kissed him softly. "You were great."

"Really?"

"Really," Sam assured him.

Gus wanted to say the three little words on the tip of his tongue, but he knew it was the wrong time. They had both indicated on a couple of occasions that they thought their feelings were heading in that direction, and that was good enough for him, for the time being.

Sam had warned Gus not to confuse lust with love, but Gus was pretty sure he knew what he was feeling, and it would all come out in due time. But for now he was just going to enjoy what they had and figure out how to make it work when they returned to the Citadel.

They settled down and spooned, with Sam backed up against Gus and Gus's arm wrapped tightly around Sam's waist, holding him close. Gus was being lulled into sleep by Sam gently brushing his fingers up and down Gus's arm, but Gus could tell Sam was still awake.

"You okay?"

"Yeah."

"You?"

"Couldn't be better."

Sam squeezed Gus's arm. "Good night, Gus."

"Night, Sam."

"Gus?"

"Yeah?"

"I know it's only been three months, but I love you."

Gus smiled. He would have bet his life that this tough, smart, and opinionated kid from Michigan who'd warned him against falling in love with his first would never have been the first to say the magic words.

Gus pulled Sam closer and kissed the back of his neck. "I love you too, Sam."

Sam turned around in Gus's arms until they were face to face. He was beaming.

Gus kissed him gently.

"I think we need to celebrate our newfound love." Sam reached down between Gus's legs.

"I think I like where this is headed."

EPILOGUE

GUS'S FAMILY returned late Monday afternoon as planned. Although that meant he and Sam didn't have the freedom to do what they wanted, they still managed to grab a moment here and there for a kiss or a touch in passing. The back of Gus's bedroom door saw some of the same action as the back of the door in their dorm room.

Thanksgiving was quite the production. Caterers arrived Wednesday afternoon and milled about making preparations. Both sides of Gus's family and most of the family law firm attended Thanksgiving dinner, held, in Southern fashion, midafternoon. After the meal, the men retired to the family room to watch ball games while the women remained in the dining room gossiping over coffee.

Sam seemed a bit bemused by the whole affair, so Gus made a point of catching his gaze and smiling as often as he reasonably could. Gus was used to all the fuss. The day went rather well except for the fact that once or twice Gus's father tried to get him to talk about his career plans, but luckily his mother intervened and his father acquiesced. Gus was cynically grateful for the presence of so many guests since it meant neither of his parents wanted any displays of friction.

Gus planned activities to keep him and Sam out of the house on Friday and Saturday, including a day at the beach four-wheeling and a tour of Charleston, during which Gus could share his love of history and his unique hometown with Sam. But almost before he knew it, it was Sunday morning and time to get back to the Citadel.

On Saturday night they excused themselves fairly early with the excuse of an early morning ahead and the need to pack, but that had nothing to do with anything. They made good use of their time by packing in a hurry, showering, and making quiet passionate love for most of the night. It would be their last chance for a while, and now that Gus knew he and Sam were in love and had something solid, he didn't care if his parents found out. He wasn't quite ready to tell them he was gay, but being intimate with Sam was so much more important than the possibility of getting caught. Unlike at the Citadel, where their love could get them expelled, the only thing his father could do was disown him. That would at least alleviate the problem of his presumed career choice. For now, however, Gus's issues with his dad were the last thing on his mind. All his thoughts were focused on Sam.

When the alarm sounded at eight o'clock the next morning, Gus and Sam had been awake for quite some time, lying quietly and simply holding on to each other. They'd made desperate love for the last time around five, not knowing if they would have the opportunity to be together again until Christmas break.

They had to report back by eleven, and they still had to fake their way through breakfast with Gus's family. Sam and Gus showered and dressed, taking as long as they could, stretching out what was left of their time together.

They were locked in an embrace when Emmy knocked on the door to tell them breakfast was ready. "We'll be down in a second," Gus said.

Gus moved Sam to the back of the door and pressed his body against Sam's. "This is it," he whispered. "When we step through this door, everything will go back to the way it was."

"Not everything," Sam said. "We now know how we feel, and we're gonna make this work."

"We have no choice," Gus said. "It's our relationship or the Citadel. Our education and dreams or our love."

"I want them all," Sam said.

"We can't have them all. At least not right now." He stepped back and turned Sam's face until they were looking into each other's eyes. "School is only for three more years. We can survive this."

"And if we don't?" Sam asked.

"Then it wasn't meant to be."

Sam buried his head in Gus's neck. "Sam! Look at me."

When their eyes met again, Gus was ready. "We can get through this. We love each other, and that won't go away. We'll do what we have to do to stay in school and keep our love alive. Okay?"

Sam nodded, smiled weakly, and held up his pinky finger. "Let's make a pact to stay together. And before you laugh, I want you to know I take my pinky pacts very seriously."

Gus smiled. "You got it."

They hooked their pinky fingers together, and Gus pulled Sam in for a slow, passionate kiss. When the kiss ended, they both picked up their duffel bags and walked through the door without another word.

They faked their way through breakfast as well as the ride back to the Citadel. When Gus's dad stopped the car at the Hagood Gate, his parents got out and they all exchanged hugs and handshakes.

"Now, Sam," Anne-Emerson said. "You will be back for Christmas, won't you?"

"Yes, ma'am. If you'll have me."

"It would be our pleasure."

Gus and Sam looked at each other, took a deep breath, and started walking toward the Hagood Gate.

"Stop!" Gus said.

"What?" Sam asked. "Did you forget something?"

"Yeah. This."

Gus threw his arm over Sam's shoulder like a buddy would, and Sam returned the gesture. Arm over arm, they walked through the Citadel gates on their own terms.

They might not be able to be who they really were for a while, but they were strong enough to follow the rules on their own terms, and who knew? Maybe over the next three years, they might just shake things up at the Military College of South Carolina.

SCOTTY CADE left Corporate America and twenty-five years of marketing and public relations in 2004 to buy an inn & restaurant on the island of Martha's Vineyard with Kell, his husband of over twenty years.

He started writing stories as soon as he could read, but only in the last five years for publication. When not at the inn, you can find him on the bow of his boat writing romance novels with his Shetland sheepdog, Mavis, at his side. Being from the South and a lover of commitment and fidelity, all of his characters find their way to long, healthy relationships, however long it takes them to get there. He believes that, in the end, the boy should always get the boy.

Scotty and Kell are avid boaters and live aboard their boat, spending the summers on Martha's Vineyard and winters in various locations down south.

Website: www.scottycade.com
Facebook: www.facebook.com/scotty.cade
Twitter: @ScottyCade
E-mail: scotty@scottycade.com

Leeland Jeffers is a contented single man with a thriving career in Atlanta. He's had a few unsuccessful relationships over the years, but no one has even come close to his first love, Harrison Rhinehart. They met in college when a mutual friend, Suzie Garrison, introduced Harry into their close-knit group. When the supposedly "straight" Harry made a move on Lee, the two men entered into a tumultuous secret love affair. In their senior year, the relationship finally ended when Harry informed Lee he was marrying Suzie.

Since graduation, the college friends have drifted apart. However, an unexpected invitation to a destination wedding seems set to reunite them all. Lee's speculation on whether Harry and Suzie will make an appearance threatens to derail his attendance. But Lee decides the hell with it and makes plans to go, Harry Rhinehart or no Harry Rhinehart.

www.dreamspinnerpress.com

Sequel to *The Royal Street Heist*
Bissonet & Cruz Investigations: Book Two

Halloween is Beau Bissonet's favorite holiday, from carving pumpkins to decorating his yard to donning a costume and scaring the neighborhood kids. But this year his Halloween is about to take a different turn, one that will challenge his skills as a detective and his commitment to his partner in work and love.

A year since Beau and Tollison solved *The Royal Street Heist*, found love, and formed Bissonet & Cruz Investigations, they are thriving personally and professionally. That is until Tollison's ex, Bastien Andros, shows up out of the blue. Naturally, Beau's suspicious, but two days after Bastien's arrival, he goes missing, and Tollison worries his past may catch up to him.

A mysterious package makes clear who has Bastien and what's at stake. With both Bastien and Beau's lives now at risk, Tollison has only one option: travel to Zurich, Switzerland, secure and deliver the ransom, keep both men safe, and stay true to himself at the same time.

www.dreamspinnerpress.com

Prequel to *Final Encore*

Tires flying over the interstate, college student Ian Dillon can't get out of Greenville, SC quickly enough. As he watches his entire life fading away in his rearview mirror, his thoughts are only of his lover, Todd, and the memories of their time together, now completely shattered by Todd's incomprehensible betrayal. His mind still reeling, Ian drives through the night until a split second decision guides him to Nashville, Tennessee. Everything will be better there. It has to be!

www.dreamspinnerpress.com

Sequel to *Before the Final Encore*

When hunky aspiring country singer Billy Eagan heads to Nashville in search of his big break, a relationship and love are the furthest things from his mind. Taking a foreman's job at the Lazy H ranch and not knowing how he will be accepted, Billy decides to fly under the radar and stay as closeted as he can without denying who he really is. It's immediately confirmed that he made the right decision when he discovers homophobia is still alive and well in Tennessee.

Then Billy gets his break and meets gorgeous record label executive Ian Dillon. Their worlds collide both professionally and personally, and Billy falls hard. But Ian is still haunted by the mysterious betrayal of his one and only lover, and knowing Billy possesses the power to emotionally destroy him, Ian decides to cut his losses and simply walk away. Determined not to give up on the man he loves, Billy secretly starts to unravel the past and quickly finds that it's not what it appears. Can Billy rescue Ian's heart, or will bigotry and hatred win over love?